The Burning

Full Disclosure Three

Ellis Logan

An Earth Lodge® Publication
Roxbury, Connecticut

Published in the U.S.A. by Earth Lodge®
Cover Design by Maya Cointreau

ISBN 978-1-944396-55-8

"Think you're escaping and run into yourself. Longest way round is the shortest way home."

- James Joyce, *Ulysses*

Chapter 1

It wasn't until I saw the telltale cables of Zakim Bridge piercing the sky over the Charles River that I realized we were about to enter Boston.

I'd assumed my brother would be taking us straight back to Montreal. Or worse, back to Aeden. I had felt the sting in Hollis' gaze, every time he seared me with his icy glare in the rearview mirror. I had suspected a tongue-lashing was imminent, but so far he had remained silent.

I suspected he had no words for what I'd done. I knew I was having a hard time processing it myself.

David's head lay warmly against my shoulder, his long sandy hair tickling my neck. Rather than brush it away, I reveled in it, proof that he was here, that we'd done it. A dream no longer, for the first time in weeks I finally had him at my side again. After he'd been taken by the warpers, I had started to doubt I would ever get him back. Even now, I wasn't sure what they'd done to him, how damaged he might be. His body would heal, but his mind? I didn't know.

For weeks, all I'd thought about was rescuing David. Seeing him safe. Finally, I had done it. I was bringing him home. But at what cost?

Every time Hollis' angry eyes flicked towards me, I feared the answer.

Too high.

I hadn't rescued David. I had traded one hostage for another. David was safe, but now Khai was at the mercy of the warpers, alien hybrids with a thirst for world domination. The boy I had known since birth, trained with since I could walk, confided in since I'd had wishes and dreams – he was gone, and it was all my fault. If I hadn't insisted on saving David myself, if I hadn't run off, none of this would have happened. Even the fact that David had been taken in the first place, if I really wanted to get down to it, even that could be traced back to my selfishness.

How had we gotten here?

How the hell had this happened?

I had wanted was to enjoy my final summer of freedom before venturing further into adulthood. I'd always lived a relatively unassuming life. It wasn't like I was asking for anything much. A month hiking the wilds of Vermont, some fun clubbing and finding an apartment, then start University with my best friends. When I'd stumbled upon a secret warper encampment hidden in the woods along the Long Trail, I had thought I could ignore the drama and finish out the hike. What was the harm, right? All I had wanted was a few quiet days, some time to finish the trail in peace. I had been stupid: dazed and distracted by my own awakening powers as a water fae. The warpers had taken their discovery as an invitation to move on their brethren, attacking the starseed headquarters in Montreal and taking David in one efficient strike.

My family had said they'd take care of it. That they'd work with the starseeds to find my boyfriend, save everyone.

They'd saved no one.

Weeks had turned into months and still David hadn't been found. I had taken matters into my own hands, fled Valhalla and dragged my friends along with me to search for David. Khai and Hollis had followed us, to stop us maybe, or help us, I don't know. They'd shown up just after we'd found David and were trying to escape the facility, the warpers hot on our tail. All I'd been thinking of, the absolute single thing on my mind, had been getting David to safety.

And that's when it had all gone horribly, terribly wrong.

David had gotten out. Everyone had gotten out. Except Khai. He'd told me to run.

I hadn't wanted to. I'd tried to help him as a horde of warpers held him down. But my powers had failed, and he'd screamed for me to run.

And gods help me, I did.

Chapter 2

Following the van's built-in GPS, Hollis navigated effortlessly through the city to pull into an unmarked basement parking garage. I had caught a quick glimpse of the building before we entered, a nondescript affair of dingy cement and blacked out windows. I'd been to Boston many times before, but I had never been here. Following Storrow Drive to River Street, I'd almost grown excited as I realized we were heading towards Cambridge, one of my favorite places in Boston. But instead, we had turned onto a small street marked Blackstone and entered an aging industrial park. Idly, I wondered who owned the building we were now under. Fae? Starseeds? I decided I didn't really care. I would find out soon enough.

Hollis got out of the van without a word, opening the back doors and hefting an unconscious Elaine over his shoulder. I shook David awake, my heart wrenching when a look of terror washed over his face.

"It's okay," I said, soothing him. "You're safe now, remember?"

Slowly, his eyes focused on mine and he nodded, exhaustion replacing the fear.

"Come on, we're here." I prayed he wouldn't ask where here was, since I had no answers. I needn't have worried. He didn't say a word as he climbed out of the van, except to mumble thanks when he stumbled and Gawen caught him.

None of us looked happy as we followed Hollis towards the elevator in the corner. Despite having found David, we were a team defeated. Jules and Reenah walked at my side, but I couldn't meet their eyes.

What had I done?

The question rocked through me again, stealing my breath. I closed my eyes, mentally willing myself to keep it together.

Jules reached down to hold my hand and I smiled weakly at a point somewhere over her right shoulder. Tears gathered in my eyes, and I looked away.

"Whatever happened, we'll make it right," she said in a low voice.

I bit my lip, not trusting myself to speak. The elevator dinged and we all got on the elevator. I noticed I wasn't the only one avoiding people's eyes. Hollis looked like he might explode at any minute, his finger punching the button for the third floor so fiercely I thought the scuffed plastic might crack.

No one said a word.

Time moved slowly, the ride upstairs lasting an eternity. When the doors opened, I released my breath. I hadn't even realized I had been holding it. If only I could have exhaled all my feelings, too.

A wide hallway stretched before us, lush red carpets, brocade-covered walls and warm copper lanterns gracing the décor. It wasn't what I would have expected. On the outside, the building had looked cold. Utilitarian. This felt more like a posh centuries-old hotel or the Harvard Club. The effect was disconcerting, making me feel like I'd teleported to another place in time. Butterflies took wing in my stomach, wings of anxiety flitting through my torso.

The hall split off to the left and right, but a large set of doors stood open across from us. A small plaque by the left door read "Conference Room 3A." Hollis strode confidently forward into the room, leaving the rest of us little choice but to follow.

Inside, a motley crew greeted us. Three adults I'd never met before. Two I had.

One of the strangers rushed forward towards David, helping Gawen lead him to a seat, while Hollis dropped Elaine onto a chair. My parents sprang forward, enveloping me in one, big, group hug.

After a moment, when it became obvious I wasn't hugging them back, they released me.

That's when the shouting began.

"By the Ancients, Ana, what were you thinking?" my dad began. I hadn't seen him scowl like that in years, not since I had fallen out of a tree when I was ten. He gripped my arms. "You could have been killed!"

"Or worse," my mom said. Her pale skin flushed, and her eyes had gone cold. "I can't believe- I never thought-" She was so angry she couldn't finish her sentences. I'd never seen her at a loss for words, and that should have scared me more than anything. "I always imagined if I had to worry about anyone, it was Hollis. Or even your father. But you. You've always been so level-headed." She slammed a fist on the large wooden table next to us and screamed. "Don't you ever, ever do anything like that again, do you hear me?" She started shaking, and her eyes became liquid. My father turned and enveloped her in his arms as she started to cry. "She could have been killed, Alec. Dammit, we could have lost her!"

"I know, Siri, I know." My father soothed her, his own voice breaking as he stroked her hair. "It's okay now. She's here, she's okay." Our eyes met over her head, and I knew he was still furious with me.

I tried to feel terrible. By the Ancients, I knew I deserved it. But my emotions had already ebbed to their lowest low. Lost in a sea of festering guilt and shock, there was nowhere for them to go. My parents' tears were mere drops in an ocean of salty regret. Sighing, knowing there was nothing I could do to change what I had done, I walked away.

Gawen was standing near David, arms crossed over his chest while he watched a grey-haired woman take David's blood pressure.

"He's fine," I said, gesturing at the cuff around his arm. "His body is, at least."

The woman ignored me, finishing the procedure and checking her results. Only then did she look up and acknowledge my presence.

"You're Ana, I take it?"

"Yes, I-"

"I understand you have healing abilities? What is your assessment?"

Her cool manner took me off guard. "He's weak, but I did all I can. They were messing with his DNA, to do what, I don't know, but I think I reversed the effects of whatever they had him on."

"I took pictures of all the medications we found," Gawen volunteered.

"Good. You can forward them to me later." She returned her attention to me. "If you've healed him, why is he still like this?"

"The damage they did to him, it's more than just physical... I don't know how to heal it. I don't even know if it even can be healed." The last part came out as a whisper. I didn't like discussing David like he wasn't there, but he didn't seem to notice. He just sat there, staring down at his hands. Annoyed, I looked back at the woman. "Who are you, anyway?"

"Sharon Schramm. I'm a doctor."

"And a starseed?" I asked.

"Yes, that too." She eyed my leg. "That looks like a gunshot on your leg, are you-"

"I'm fine," I cut her off.

"A gunshot!" I hadn't realized my mother was standing right behind us. "Let me see."

Instead of kneeling, she put a hand on my shoulder. Like me, my mother could heal most wounds. I could feel her scanning my body, a prickling sensation I'd never noticed in my youth. I could only assume my increased sensitivity had to do with my new water abilities. The sensation of being scanned was like being tickled lightly with a thousand tiny eyelashes. Not unpleasant, but not comfortable, either. I felt her probing the place on my thigh where Cougan's bullet had split the skin. I'd already set the wound to healing on the ride here. The bleeding had stopped long before, the sting of the seared edges gone. Satisfied that the wound needed no further attention, my mom squeezed my shoulder and dropped her hand.

"She's okay," she affirmed.

"I told you I was."

"Not a word out of you." She spun to point a finger ferociously at me. "You don't get to do that. Not here. Not today."

"Do what?" I asked before I could stop myself.

"Have attitude. Act like you know best. Like you know anything. Because you don't." Her eyes lasered through me as only a mom's could.

"You're right. I'm sorry," I said without real feeling.

I sighed and took the seat next to David. I reached out and took his hands in mine, but he still didn't look up. I was tempted to probe his aura, but I didn't have the courage. I wasn't sure I wanted to see what he was feeling. Already, in the van, I had felt how terribly empty and broken he was inside. I knew that wouldn't go away anytime soon. All I could do was be here for him. "Whatever you need," I whispered. "I'm here for you."

Dr. Schramm said something to my mother and then placed a hand on David's arm. When she spoke to him, her voice was different, softer. "David, I'd like you to come with me."

"Why?" he said, looking up for the first time. "Are you going to run tests on me?"

I could tell he was trying to be strong, and failing miserably.

"Not today, no. More than anything, I think you need rest."

"I don't know." His voice was thin. Weak.

"I think it's a good idea," I said, encouraging him. "Get settled in, sleep a bit more. I'll come see you in a little while."

I looked up at the doctor, daring her to challenge me, but she didn't. "Yes, that's a grand idea," she said, helping him stand. "He'll be on the fifth floor, room 522."

"Okay, thank you."

She nodded and led David from the room. As soon as she left, one of the other strangers clapped his hands, making me jump.

He was tall, dark-skinned, grey-haired with a military bearing. "Alright, I think it's past time that we get this party started. Could everyone take a seat?"

He waited for everybody to sit and then introduced himself. "My name is Doug Rice. Before you ask, I'm not a starseed, and I'm not fae. But I do have an interest in this situation, and as some as you already know, Director Carmichael has been kind enough to lend me control of her resources here." He gestured at the woman to his left and she nodded with a smile that didn't relieve the tension around her eyes. "My husband, like your friend David, was also taken in Montreal. I can only hope and assume that you might have seen him in Salem. What can you tell us?"

He looked at Hollis expectantly but my brother shook his head. "I didn't see much of anything. By the time we got there, Ana and her friends were already coming out. Khai and I just lent a hand."

"The young man who was taken?"

"Yes," Hollis said, glaring at me.

"Maybe we should start at the beginning," Doug said. He sounded serene, matter-of-fact. He would have made a great lawyer. "Ana, can you walk us through the events of the last twenty-four hours?"

I swallowed. "Sure. I guess the best place to start is in Montreal. Gawen and I were able to combine our water abilities tap into the memories of the building, see what had happened when the warpers attacked."

"Your family, did they work with the Guard?" My father interrupted, looking at Gawen.

"Yes, sir. My grandparents, Griffin and Mary Black. They were Light Guard consultants."

"Thought so. Fine people. You look just like Griffin. So, you were able to teach Ana how to see as a team? I'm impressed. That's very advanced stuff."

"Thank you, sir," Gawen blushed.

My father grunted and waved a hand towards me. "Go on, Ana. What did you see?"

"Everything," I said dully. "We saw them taking the people outside, loading them into a box truck. That woman there, Elaine, she mind-warped everyone into obeying her. Well, almost everyone. There were some people who were able to resist her. But they couldn't fight the rest of the thugs she had with her. The director, he tried to fool them but-"

"The Director? Do you mean Cliff?" Doug broke in.

"Yeah, that was his name. You know him?"

"I'm his husband."

"He said you wouldn't rest until you found him," Gawen said.

"What happened to him?"

"They took him." I shrugged. "Like everyone else. But the guy who took him, Phineas, he mentioned they were going to Salem. So we went there, too. The whole time, David kept sending me dreams, except I didn't know if they were him or just me, getting my hopes up. Luckily, the dreams were real. We were able to piece together the clues from my dreams with our research at the library to find the warper's lair."

"That's pretty impressive," Doug mused. "Thirty years ago, I would have said you should consider joining the

Navy to work with my JAG team. Not much need for that kind of thing anymore, though."

"JAG?" I asked, confused.

"Judge Advocate General Corps, the military's legal division. Time was, we could have used more people with your detective skills."

I smiled. So he had been a lawyer, after all. "Thanks." My smile faded remembering fighting the warpers, watching them swarm Khai, running from Cougan and his gun. "But I think I'm made for more peaceful pursuits."

Hollis snorted in disbelief, but Doug nodded. "I understand completely. So tell me. Did you see him? Cliff, was he there in Salem?"

I shook my head. "I don't know. I think everyone was there, but I couldn't say for sure. We only saw one small room, like a hospital ward, where they had everyone hooked up to IVs. Cliff wasn't there, but from the way Phineas talked, I think the place was much bigger than what we saw." I looked at my mom. "Mom, they said they had fae there. They've found a way to block our powers from working, block the light. They say the fae there are aging like normal people."

My mom's face grew stormy. "Over my dead body. I didn't go through everything I went through at your age just so a group of power-hungry bas-"

My dad placed a hand over hers and the effect was instantaneous. Her face cleared, and she swallowed whatever she'd been about to say.

"I think what Siri means to say is that we are going to get everyone back. Every last person."

"There were kids there, too," Gawen said. "Little kids. What kind of monster experiments on kids?"

"The worst kind," my dad muttered. I knew he was probably remembering his own little sister, murdered so many years ago by the Dark Fae.

"There's just one thing I'd like to know," Hollis said, clearing his throat. "Ana, what happened to Khai?"

The whole room looked at me at once. Eight pairs of eyes waiting for a good explanation.

If only I'd had one.

"It was after you and Gawen took David upstairs. All those people – I couldn't just leave them. Khai convinced me we had to go, and I knew he was right. We had no weapons, and my powers had already faded in the short time we'd been there. We were about to go, when these soldiers, they came out of the elevator and started attacking us. They all ganged up on Khai." The memory left a foul taste in my mouth. "Like I wasn't worth worrying about. I took out the one guy who'd tried to restrain me, but Khai was trying to fight off six or seven of them. He told me to go, and I wasn't going to. I was going to help him. I could see his powers weren't working, either. Then Cougan – do you remember that warper whose leg I broke on the Long Trail?"

Hollis nodded, swallowing.

"He had a gun. He came at me, running, and Khai screamed at me to run. Gods help me, I did. I should have stayed, but I ran."

"If you'd stayed, you'd have been captured, too. Maybe we all would. We would've come back to see what was taking you so long." It wasn't quite forgiveness, but Hollis didn't sound so angry at me anymore. I wondered how he could get there so quickly. I knew I was still a long way away.

"I guess. I don't know anything anymore. Anyways, that's what happened."

I looked around the room. Jules was holding a fist to her mouth, something she'd always done when she was too scared or angry to speak. My dad looked grim, and Gawen was holding Reenah's hand. My mom wiped a tear from her cheek. "Ana, you know we-"

"It's been a really, really long day. I'd like to check on David now. Can I go?"

I directed the question at Doug and he nodded.

"Thanks." I pushed away from the table, unable to be in the presence of my family or friends any longer.

Chapter 3

Talking about what happened had brought everything back. I'd thought unloading might be a relief, but it wasn't. I felt a hundred times worse. I wasn't sure how that was even possible, but there it was.

I'd used David as an excuse to escape the room, so I decided to follow through and head up to the fifth floor. When the elevator dinged, my body went into fight or flight mode as it remembered the fight with warpers. I told myself to stop being such a ninny and stepped inside. Moments later, I was in another finely appointed hallway, this one decorated in soothing tones of blue. I found David's room and knocked gently. I guess it hadn't been latched tight, because the door swung open with the light pressure.

Lying amid a dark blue sea of bedding, David looked pale and small. Like a boy, not the man I knew him to be. Not wanting him to pick up on what I was seeing, I pasted a brave smile on my face and breezed into the room.

"Alone at last." I climbed onto the four-poster bed next to him and leaned back against the pillows so that we were shoulder to shoulder. I picked up his hand and kissed it, sending a small stream of energy into him even as I did so. I laid my head on his shoulder and sighed happily, like I didn't have a care in the world. "You starseeds sure know how to live it up."

I cringed inwardly, even as the words left my mouth. I'd been referring to the opulent setting, but what if I'd reminded him of the warpers?

David, however, didn't seem to find anything amiss. "It is nice here, isn't it? I stayed here once before I hit the Long Trail. Our HQ down in Baltimore isn't nearly so swanky."

"No? I bet it's still nice."

"Well sure," he said, leaning his head against mine. "Pretty much everything connected to the Gregors is nice."

"Makes you wonder why the warpers think they have it better. They don't even have a good decorator," I joked before I could stop myself.

David laughed weakly. "You're right. They kind of suck at hospitality."

For a moment, we both just lay there. Him, thinking gods knew what; me, staring out the window at the Charles River winding around Allston across the way.

"I'm really sorry it took me so long to get to you," I said. "I wanted to look for you from day one, but my family wouldn't let me. They promised they would find you, but-"

David shushed me, putting a finger to my lips. "Don't. Just don't. Your parents were right. You shouldn't have come for me. It was too dangerous. The only thing that kept me from going crazy in there was the thought that they didn't have you, too."

"I know what you mean. There wasn't a day I wasn't thinking of you. When I started seeing you in dreams, I didn't know if it was really you, or if you were dead, or what. Without those dreams, I never would have found you. Well, the dreams, and my friends," I admitted.

"Your friends. Did I hear right, back there in the van? Is Khai really...?" David's voice was fading, and I looked at him. His eyelids were drooping, his gaze unfocused. Any minute now he'd be dropping off again.

"Yeah. They have him."

David exhaled, his thin frame shaking from the effort. "That could have been you." He shook his head, sounding upset.

"It should have been me," I retorted dully. Already asleep, David did not respond. I slid off the bed and tiptoed out of the room, closing the door firmly behind me.

For a moment, I stood in the hall, unsure of what to do next. I could wander the halls, but eventually I'd have to see my family again. I decided to bite the bullet and head back downstairs.

Again, the ding of the elevator surprised me, and again, I relived my last moments with Khai as I rode downstairs. When the doors opened, I expected to see an empty hallway. Instead, my father stood there with two strong-looking men and one very angry looking white haired woman.

Elaine.

A growl rose up in my throat and I lunged forward. "You!"

My father grabbed me before my fist could make contact with her face. He looked shocked, and I couldn't blame him. I hardly recognized myself. Elaine laughed, a rich throaty sound, and fear knotted in my stomach.

"Dad, her voice. You took off her gag? You can't, she'll-"

"Aw, don't worry honey. These kind gentlemen here have clipped my wings." She winked at me. "Imagine, using a warper serum against their own kind."

"What is she talking about?" I hissed.

"Apparently the warpers developed something decades ago that could block starseed abilities."

"The Gregors stole it from us," Elaine snarled. "Still think they're so perfect now?"

"Please," I scoffed. ""You're a blight on your race. If I'd known, I would've given you the shot myself."

Elaine assessed me coolly. "I'll remember you said that, honey."

I shrugged. "I saw what you did to those people in Montreal. How you treated them. They begged you. And you laughed in their faces."

She sniffed. "They deserved it."

"You think? I don't know, it looked like some of them cared about you. What was that guy's name? Marcus?"

Elaine blanched, her face becoming as pale as her hair.

"Yeah, I thought so. Do you really think he deserves to be hurt this badly? You have a chance to make it right. Change things. Tell us where your friends have gone."

Elaine looked at me, her lips soft and parted as if she wanted to say something. I could see it in her aura. She was ready to tell us. And then the light around her went black and her mouth twisted into a sneer.

"Why would I tell you anything? You'll pretend you're grateful, but we both know the Gregors won't just let me go. No, I have to pay, right boys?" The men stood at her sides, gripping her arms as they regarded her impassively. "See? Hearts of stone," she drawled.

"You should go," my father said softly. "Leave her to us. We'll find Khai and the others."

"That same old song?" I said, looking my father in the face. I shook his arms from me. "I've heard it before."

"Ana!"

"No, Dad. Not this time. Not again. I'm not leaving anything up to you. If you had found David, maybe, just maybe, I would trust you now. And maybe Khai wouldn't have been taken. But you gave up. You didn't try hard enough. Right now, I'm not sure I can forgive you."

"Oh, that's rich, isn't it?" Elaine barked with laughed. "You want me to forgive my old pals, but you can't even forgive your own father."

"Shut up," my dad and I both told her at the same time. Somehow, that just made her laugh harder. My dad punched the elevator button on the wall, calling it back.

"This isn't over, Ana. We're going to talk about this, okay?" He ran a hand through his jet-black hair, messing it up even worse than it already was.

"Whatever," I said. Instead of heading back toward the conference room, I slammed open the steel door to the stairwell and made for the great outdoors.

Chapter 4

I knew we were close to the Charles, so I headed towards the river. In no time at all, I found myself on a beautiful walking trail. Marsh grasses and the river on one side, dense evergreen plantings and tall bushes along the other; one could almost imagine they weren't in the city. Almost. The sound of cars zooming by on Memorial beyond the trees was a constant. But there were other noises, too – the water lapping gently against the banks, birds fighting over the last of the berries on bushes. Every now and then a cyclist or hoverboarder would pass by, quietly alerting me to their presence with an "On your left."

I walked for over a mile, the activity warming me up despite the chill of the season. I didn't allow myself to think, just focused on moving. Counting my breaths helped. 1-2-3-in. 1-2-3-out. The afternoon sun glittered on the surface of the river, beckoning like a siren. If only the water had been as warm as it looked: I would have dove straight in. As it was, I contented myself with a seat near the water's edge, scrambling down a small dirt track to sit on a large flat rock. Names had been carved into the hard grey surface. I wasn't the first one here, and surely wouldn't be the last. How many of us had come seeking solace or solitude?

How many had found it?

I puffed out my cheeks, trying to banish the gloom from my brain. I focused on the arc of glitter and light spanning the river, allowing myself to be mesmerized by the dancing stars along its surface. If I let my imagination go, I could almost hear their music, like a symphony of seashells tinkling in the wind.

Closing my eyes, I leaned my head back and basked in the sunshine. It was warm here by the river, sheltered from the northern wind. Comfortable, something I hadn't been in a long, long time. I knew it would probably be cold, but something made me want to put my feet in the water, like a mini baptism or something. I was so ready for a rebirth. Ready to start anew.

I unlaced my insulated high-top sneakers and peeled off my socks. Last, I rolled my pants up a couple times and stretched out my legs, slowly submerging my feet. The water was icy cold, in a delicious sort of way. I let my lids fall again and took a deep breath, ready to exhale all the bad.

"Welcome, young one," a voice whispered in my ear, making my breath catch.

Surprised, I looked around. "Who's there?" I called out, my own voice tremulous.

The voice tittered. "We are. We are always here."

"Who? What do you want?"

"It is you who have come to us. We want nothing of you." The voice sounded superior now, maybe even offended. That's when it dawned on me.

"Elementals?"

"Yes, you are the fae, we are the faerie. The spirits of the earth. We make the wind blow, the water flow, the earth rise and the flowers bloom."

"Really? I thought you were more myth than reality. Isn't it Anansanna that makes the earth alive?"

"Anansanna made us, made the earth, made you. We three go hand in hand. You are not the only ones who rode the golden ship through the stars. We came, too. We are the record keepers, beings without time nor end. We see all, know all, do all. Without us, there is no connection to make with the water, no fuel from the sun. We are the pathways that bind the world of energy and light. If you want, you could call us your co-creators."

"You know all? See all? But you just said you are always here."

"Yes, we are here. We are the keepers of this river and these lands. But we are also connected to everything else. We connect. We play." More tittering. "Sometimes we even gossip."

"Then do you know what happened to my friend, Khai Mirro? He was taken, along with many other people, from Salem by a group of bad starseeds. Not fae or faerie like us – other aliens. Do you know what I am talking about? Do you know where they might have went?"

Silence greeted me. I waited, but there was no response, no answer. After a minute, I grew frustrated and started to dry off my feet. "I guess you don't know everything," I muttered.

I was just about to stand and leave when the voice surprised me.

"Do not be so quick to judge us, faeling. Knowledge cannot be timed. There is no race to wisdom, only eternal acceptance."

"Okay... Is there something you can tell me? Anything?"

"Indeed. We have talked among ourselves, and we have seen something. Some ones. We do not know if it is your friend, but there are more fae upstream, unhappy ones. And there are others – not like us, not like you. Yet nor human. We also sense fae and others in a group towards the sea, but they are less unhappy, less angry-"

"That's probably where I came from, the starseed headquarters here in Boston. There are good people there. Not like us, but not bad."

"We remember these star people you talk of. There used to be many more of them here on the planet. There was a very bad war. Terrible. Most of them died, or left. We do not connect with them. The few who are left, they are not like us. Not like you or like we or your human brethren. Are you sure you want to meet more of them?"

The voice seemed to think it was a bad idea, but I needed to know. "Yes. I am sure. I need to save my friend. All those people who are unhappy – I need to rescue them. Can you tell me where they are?"

"They sit in a large building by the water. The walls look like frozen water, holding all the colors of the rainbow."

"Um, okay. Rainbow walls, got it. Is there anything nearby? Anything else you can tell me?" My heart sped up in my chest, fueled by anticipation.

"The building has a dock in the river, and three large boats at rest. The bad people, they like to take the boats out on our surface and hunt our fish for sport. They do not eat what they catch, and they often toss their trash in the water. We do not like them."

"No, I don't imagine you do," I murmured. "I can't say I do, either."

I stood up and dusted off my pants.

"Thanks for talking to me. You've been a big help, and given me a lot to think about."

"You will go now?" The voice whispered, sounding both afraid and excited. Find these people? Find your friends?"

"Yes."

This time, I wouldn't do it alone. I'd already acted impulsively once and paid the price. No, it was time to storm the castle, which meant I needed an army.

Chapter 5

First, though, what I really needed was dinner. By the time I got back to HQ, the sun was setting. My friends were sitting in the lobby's lounge area. The girls were both watching an old superhero movie on a large holo-screen while Reenah braided Jules' hair. Gawen was sprawled across one entire couch, snoring lightly.

"Ana, you're back!" Jules exclaimed. She made to move and Reenah tugged her back by her hair.

"Nuh-uh, not done yet," Reenah scolded. Then she turned her surly gaze on me. "We were starting to worry about you. Thought you'd gone off all Lone Ranger or some crap."

"No," I said, sinking onto a nearby chair. "I'm done with that. We're a team, remember?"

"Good," Reenah said sagely. "Just making sure you remember, too."

"You're gonna make a great mom someday, you know that?" I teased.

"I've had enough practice." She looked over at Gawen and grinned. "Sometimes it's like having a puppy."

Right on cue, Gawen whimpered slightly and rolled over, onto his side. He reached for a blanket to cover himself, like he was cold, but only succeeded in pulling his tee-shirt up past his abs.

We burst out laughing and Gawen sat up quickly, rubbing his chest. "What is it? What's happening? Oh, hey Ana."

He went from dazed, to worried, to relaxed again in less than five seconds, making me crack up even harder.

"Finished," Reenah said, patting Jules' hair. She'd woven several cornrows above Jules' left ear.

"That's pretty bad-ass," I said, admiring Reenah's handiwork.

"Thanks," Reenah said. "Gawen, you're up next. I'm tired of that man-bun thing you've got going on lately."

"Whatever. If you insist. Think we can get a bite to eat first? I'm starved."

"Yeah," said Jules. "Let's go check out the caf."

"There's a cafeteria?" I raised an eyebrow.

"Yeah, down the hall. Hungry?"

"Starved. Let's eat."

Turns out, the caf was amazing. Way better than anything I'd experienced at school, the dining hall had a whole kitchen staff ready to make whatever you wanted from a menu posted on the wall. You placed your order, took a numbered wooden chip, and then waited for your number to be posted on a screen. I watched some people pick up their orders and inhaled the heavenly aromas coming from the kitchen. Everything looked amazing. How was a girl to choose? In the end, I ordered a chocolate shake, some vegetarian Shepard's pie and a strawberry cobbler and sat down to wait with my friends at a table in the corner.

I'd just gotten my food and was starting to dig in when a beautiful, dark-skinned older woman made her way to our table.

"Ana Alvarsson?" She asked in a melodious voice, looking at me. She carried herself with grace, but she was dressed more like someone my own age in tight brown leather pants and a plum cardigan sweater that did nothing to hide the faded, battle-worn concert tee underneath. Her hair was long, a salt-and-pepper affair streaked with rich purple and raspberry highlights.

"Um, yes?" I put down my shake and wiped my mouth with the back of one hand.

"Do you mind if I sit?" She gestured at the space across from me where Jules had been sitting until her number was called.

"Knock yourself out," I said, shrugging. Her eyes were a strange golden hue that made me feel hunted. Or maybe it was just the fact that she had specifically come over looking for me. Yeah, that could have been it.

"I'm Calliope Winters. I'm hoping we can be friends." She smiled at me warmly.

"Okay," I said. "Well, I'm Ana. This is Gawen Black and Reenah Shin. And that's Jules Harrison." I pointed to where Jules was putting ketchup on her burger.

"Your parents said it was okay for me to come find you, I hope you don't mind. The thing is, I hear you've seen my friend, Cliff Collet."

The blood drained from my face. "Calliope. You're Callie?"

"You've heard of me?"

I swallowed, looking at Gawen for backup.

He'd been monitoring our conversation with split interest, half his attention on devouring the potato skins in front of him.

"We both have," he confirmed, leaning back and draping an arm over Reenah's chair. He eyed Callie with a deceptively relaxed air. "Before the warpers took him, Cliff warned them you'd come after them. They didn't care."

"No, I imagine they wouldn't. Warpers don't care about much," she said with a sigh. "Was he hurt?"

"Not that we saw," Gawen said. "There's no telling, now though."

Callie grimaced. "No. We just have to hope for the best, like always. He's stronger than he looks, Cliff."

"Phineas called you a traitor. What did he mean?" I asked. Jules had returned to the table and eyed Callie with interest.

Her amber gaze locked on mine again and I recoiled. I'd been thinking that Phineas was right, that this woman wasn't scary at all, but suddenly I realized I'd underestimated Calliope Winters. She'd seen things. She knew things. Worse. She'd done things.

"Let's just say I wasn't blessed with the kind of loving birth family you were. My grandfather was a warper. A powerful one. I didn't meet him until I was older than you are now, and when I did, he tried to make me join his cause."

"What happened?" Reenah asked, leaning forward with her chin in her hands.

"I refused," Callie said airily. "As you can imagine, that didn't go over so well. Which kind of brings me to why I'm here. I don't know where the warpers are. Even if I did, I'm a bit old to go charging into a fight." She smiled sunnily around the table. "I promised my husband I'll sit this one out, see? But that doesn't mean I don't care. I needed to be here. I care about Cliff a lot, he's my best friend. He's always had my back, and I've always had his."

"Kind of like how we have Ana's," Jules said, leaning over and squeezing my wrist.

"Exactly like that, yes. Which is good, because I recognize that look in her eye." She pierced me again with her molten gaze.

"You do?" I squeaked.

"I do. Cliff used to get it, too, right before he'd drag me off on some honor's duty. Every time, it was the right thing to do. And every time, people told us we were crazy. I can't tell you how often we almost died."

I swallowed. This wasn't really anything I wanted to hear. I didn't need to be scared. I was already terrified. It didn't matter. It wouldn't change a thing. Callie nodded as if she'd heard me.

"I know you won't change your mind. That's not why I'm here. I may be a mom, but I'm not your mom."

"How do you know that? I didn't say-"

"Please. Starseed, remember? You broadcast your thoughts like a drive-in theatre. You might want to practice blocking them."

"How can we do that?" Reenah asked.

"It's different for everyone. Some people imagine a barrier around their head. Some people imagine a wall of white noise or concrete blocks. Me, the only thing that used to work was to pick a song I really liked, and just sing it over and over again on repeat in my head. Made everybody else crazy, but to me it was just background noise."

"Huh." I mulled it over. I wasn't really into music. Gawen spoke up.

"Ana, you can probably use the same techniques you use for auric shielding. Try it out."

I scrunched up my lips, thinking. "It should work." I looked at Callie. "You tell me."

I raised my shields and started daydreaming about riding Ayita, my unicorn back home. It had been months since I'd seen her, and I sincerely hoped she was getting enough activity without me to ride her every day.

After a minute, I looked at Callie. "Well?"

"Nothing. You're a total blank."

"Awesome!" Gawen high-fived me. "We'll just have to make sure we shield before we meet any more warpers.

Callie crossed her arms, leaning back in her seat. "More than that. You should be shielded anytime you think you might be anywhere near some danger. Otherwise, a good reader can hear you from over a block away."

"Damn, really?" Gawen looked impressed.

"Really," she said. Her chat pinged and she looked at it. "That's my husband, Ethan, wondering where I am. He's sure I'm going to get myself into trouble. It's not his fault, I usually do. Anyhoo, like I said, I came over for a reason. I wanted to give you something."

She reached into her pocket, drawing out a small sparkling object. She placed it on the table and we all leaned forward, looking at it.

"What is it?" Jules asked in a hushed voice.

It looked like a stone, like a small shard of opal about the size of my pinky toe, but it glimmered like it was alive. I leaned in closer, sure that I had just seen what looked like a shooting star flare across its surface to disappear within a shifting nebula.

"It's not a stone," I asserted, though I had no idea what else it could be.

"It is, and it's not. What you are looking at is a small piece of the Star Mother."

"The what now?" Gawen asked, looking up from the stone.

"The Star Mother. An ancient stone pillar left behind by the Nommo."

"The aliens," I supplied.

"My ancestors, yes. The Star Mother was in my possession for many years. The Nommo spoke to me often through it, and it allowed me to do a lot of great things. It's part of the reason the warpers were so quiet for the better part of thirty years – they knew I could always find them, stop them, while I had it."

"And you lost it?" Jules asked, incredulous.

"I did," Callie said, chuckling. How she could laugh about it, I had no idea. Again, I decided she was scarier than she looked. "The warpers stole the stone five years ago. This is one of the few pieces I have left. Even such a small piece, it's powerful. It can augment starseed powers. Whatever you do, don't lose it."

"Why would you give this to me?" I asked. Inside, I was afraid. Another responsibility. Another way to mess up.

"Because you have the same look in your eye that Cliff would always get. I used to call it the hero's look. Ethan just called it trouble." Again, she laughed. "God, we had some good times. I don't know if the stone can help you. The Nommo, they haven't talked to me since the Star Mother was stolen, not through this," she held up a shimmering opalescent ring for me to look at, "or that piece. Still. I know your family has earth powers. Maybe one of you can wake it up. I don't know. It just seemed like it was time to pass it on. I always trust my gut."

"Does it work?" I asked.

"The stone?"

"No, your gut."

Callie smirked. "Usually. Most of the time. I'm a starseed, not a psychic."

She pushed away from the table, standing. She looked down at all of us, the smile fading from her face.

"But I do know one thing. You're not going to rest until you get your people back, and that means my people, too. Just, try not to lose yourself in the process, okay?" She quirked an eyebrow at me. "You've got a lot of anger and guilt swirling around in there, I've seen it. Don't let it get the better of you."

And then, she was walking away. The stone on the table shone, beautiful to look at. I picked it up, turning it over in my hand.

"I forgot to ask why they called it the Star Mother."

"Eh. Probably just because of how it looks," Gawen said, going back to shoveling food into his mouth.

"I guess," I said, pocketing the small rock. It felt warm in my pocket. Alive. Callie must have been carrying it in her own pants before giving it to me.

Shaking off the weirdness of what had just happened, I went back to eating. There'd be time later for plotting, guessing and planning.

Chapter 6

After finishing up at the caf, we wandered back out into the lobby.

"So, what should we do now?" Jules asked. "Seems too early to go back to our rooms."

"Rooms?" I asked.

"Yeah, they gave us all rooms," Gawen said. "It's like a five-star hotel up there on the fourth floor, I swear. Apparently all the big wigs have quarters on the third floor, along with the conference rooms, and visitors and trainees are on the fourth and fifth. Health services are up on the fifth, too, and all the training rooms are on the second and first."

"I was up on the fifth. It was nice. Do you know where my room is?"

They all looked at each other.

"What?"

"You're sharing a room with your parents. A suite, actually."

I rolled my eyes. "Figures. I'm surprised they let me out of their sight this long."

"Well, we don't have to go back. I mean, we're in Boston. Maybe we should go check out the local clubs," Jules suggested.

"Man. Aren't you tired?" Reenah asked. "I'm beat. Anything less than six hours sleep and I'm useless."

"Tell me about it," Gawen said with a grin. "Sleeping Beauty here hates waking up before ten."

She swatted him. "You're one to talk."

"Hey, I function just fine without sleep. Doesn't mean I don't enjoy it. Naps are good for the soul."

I smiled, watching them bicker.

"I'd love to go clubbing, I really would." Jules' eyes lit up and I held up my hand. "But I can't. I have to talk to my parents. To you guys, too."

"Why? What's up?" Gawen's demeanor switched from teasing to concerned in a flash.

"I might have a lead on the warpers."

"What?! How?" Jules exclaimed.

"It's kind of a long story. Let's go find my parents, that way I can tell everybody at once. We should probably find Hollis, too. Not that he wants to see me, I'm sure," I groused.

"You leave Hollis to me," Jules said. "I'll make sure he's there. I'm pretty sure he's working out on the second floor, I'll go get him. Meet you in room 438 in five."

She stalked off towards the stairs.

"Okay," I drawled. "What's going on?"

Reenah shook her head, looking perplexed. "I'm not sure. I haven't seen Hollis since we got here. After you left, we all went to our rooms to clean up. When we met down in the lobby, Jules was all worked up but she insisted nothing was wrong."

Gawen snorted. "She's a terrible liar."

"I know," I said, giggling. "She really is."

"Her aura was so twisted. Like Jackson Pollack on a really, really off day," he said.

"Oh, that's bad."

"I know, right?"

Reenah cocked her head to one side. "I'm not sure if I should be jealous or grateful that I'm not a water fae."

"Grateful," I said.

Gawen spoke at the same time. "Jealous."

Reenah laughed. "Well, that clears everything up." She shook her head. "Come on. Let's go find your parents. I'm dying to hear your story."

She grabbed my hand and dragged me towards the elevators. Up on the fourth floor, we had to turn several corners to find my suite, room 438. I tried the knob. Locked. Since I didn't have a key, I had to knock. While I was waiting, I looked at my friends.

"So, is Hollis staying in here, too?"

Reenah shook her head. "I think he has his own room, like us."

"Figures," I mumbled.

My mother opened the door and smiled at all of us. "Hey kids! Ana, lovely of you to grace us with your presence."

"Like I had a choice." I know I needed to just get with the program, but just seeing my mom, knowing that I had to share a room with my parents like a little kid, brought all my teen angst back up to the surface. My mom responded with a well-executed eye roll of her own and stepped aside to let us into the posh suite. Everything was decorated in warm hues of sunny golds and rich pine. The carpet was thick and plush, like a freshly harvested hay field. "These are my friends, Gawen Black and Reenah Shin."

"Yes, we had ample time to become acquainted after you disappeared from the meeting this afternoon."

Okay. Clearly, my mother was still upset with me.

"Right, yeah. I'm sorry about that. I was kind of overwhelmed."

My mother eyed me up and down. "And now you're feeling better? Because that's all that matters."

I blinked. I couldn't tell if she was being sarcastic or not. There was an edge to her voice that I wasn't familiar with.

"I feel better, yeah." I decided to just go with it, act like no one was mad at each other. I didn't have time for niceties. I needed to get back down to business.

My mother raised her eyebrows.

"Okay. Why don't you all sit down? I was just about to make some hot chocolate."

Mom had always held chocolate in high esteem, putting it up there with sunshine and exercise for its health benefits. Of course, she would have made sure her room was well stocked with the necessary ingredients for life. It was a minor obsession that seemed to have been handed down from mother to daughter through generations of Alvarssons. I looked around.

"Where's Dad?"

"He should be out any minute. He just went in to take a shower. Why, was there something that you, maybe, oh I don't know, wanted to say to us? An apology perhaps?"

Mom's voice was dry and breezy. This time, the sarcasm was impossible to miss.

"That's exactly what I want to do, apologize." It hadn't actually been on my to-do list, but since she'd brought it up I figured I better proceed as recommended. If my mom wanted an apology, she should get one. Not just because it would smooth things over between us – because she deserved one. True, my parents had locked me away in Valhalla. They had treated me like a child, and it had made me angry, made me act out in ways that I shouldn't have. Things could have gone better. Should have gone better. I wasn't the only one at fault, but I could own up to the mistakes I'd made.

My mother looked surprised. Obviously, she hadn't been expecting me to fess up so quickly.

"Right, okay. I'll just get these mugs put together. If you need anything, Ana, your room is right over there." She pointed to a door in the corner by a huge window overlooking the river. I thought about getting cleaned up but figured I'd better wait until my dad came out. I could always change after we talked. After all, a sudden preoccupation with my cleanliness would be the perfect out if the conversation got too heated.

"Okay, thanks," I said, sitting between Reenah and Gawen on the couch. None of us relaxed, not even when my mother brought us our hot cocoas.

"Thank you, Mrs. Alvarsson," Reenah said nervously. Gawen just picked up his mug and inhaled deeply like he was trying to soothe his nerves. When my mom went back to the kitchenette he leaned over towards me and whispered in my ear.

"You guys have really similar energy signatures, do you know that?"

I'd never really thought of myself being anything like my mom. Tall, beautiful, graceful. Even at fifty years old, she'd remained a prime athlete and crush fodder for most of the boys at my school. I shook my head.

"Thanks?"

"Really, you do. I can see she's just really worried about you. She loves you a lot."

I looked at my mom, concentrated on adjusting my own energy so that I could see her aura. Gawen was right. Her energy was agitated, angry-looking, but it was also filled with a pink light that showed that everything she was doing came from a place of love.

"I better keep this thing turned on," I muttered to Gawen under my breath.

Gawen nodded. "People's auras can be a real eye-opener, you know? People's words and emotions can have a real disconnect. So often, people are coming from a better place than we know."

Reenah, having heard most of our conversation, grumbled into her own cup. "Yeah, unless those people are warpers and then it's a lot worse than you would think."

"Amen sister," I said, clinking mugs with her. Someone knocked at the door and then it swung open. Hollis strode in, followed by Jules. So much for Hollis having his own room. But of course, it made sense. Another guard to watch over poor, misguided Ana. Whatever. I needed to let go of my anger. I was the one who'd asked Jules to find him. I had no right to be annoyed now that he was here, even if teasing me seemed to have been his life's mission since the day I was born.

Brothers.

You just had to hope that one day they'd grow up, or grow away.

My mother rushed to greet them, a decidedly more friendly expression on her face than the one she'd met us with.

"Come in, come in. I was just getting everyone settled with some cocoa. Sit down and I'll join you in a minute."

Hollis sat on the couch across from me, folding his arms over his brawny chest and fixing me with a stare. It wasn't hostile, per se, but it wasn't friendly, either. More like, he wanted to see how I was going to dig myself out of the hole I was in.

I bit my lip, stifling a grin. He wasn't the only one. Hollis' presence had the natural sibling effect of making me feel feistier, and I welcomed the sassiness blooming within. Somehow, I knew I'd need it in the days to come. But I also knew I shouldn't piss off my family any more than I already had, so I tried to keep my feelings to myself.

It didn't work, of course. Hollis had always been able to see through me like glass. Maybe he had a bit of water fae to him, as well.

"What's so funny?" he asked.

"Nothing." I smirked.

He sighed. "Brat."

"Ogre," I said, lifting my eyebrows and sticking out my tongue.

"That's enough, you two," my mother said by rote, handing Jules and Hollis their mugs.

A familiar, deep voice rang clear through the chatter. "Am I hearing the angelic sing-song voices of my children?"

Chapter 7

My dad sauntered into the room, toweling off his jet black hair with just a pair of sweats hanging on his lean frame.

Reenah sat up and started coughing on her drink, while I leaned over and rubbed her back. Quickly, I looked over at my dad.

"We've got guests. Think you could maybe put some clothes on?"

Oblivious as usual to the effect he had on women of all ages, my dad rolled his deep violet eyes. "I'm dressed."

I looked at my mom, pleading for some backup.

"This isn't training, Alec. Go put on a shirt," she chided gently.

"Fine, fine." He disappeared back into the Master Bedroom only to return moments later, pulling an army-green tank top over his torso. Not a total improvement, but it was better than nothing. I eyed Reenah, who was staring intently down into her near-empty mug. It wasn't the first time I'd seen a peer geek out over my dad's hotness. I was sure it wouldn't be the last. He may have been in his mid-fifties, but he didn't even look thirty by human standards. Sometimes, it creeped even me out.

Gawen cleared his throat and stood, walking over to introduce himself and Reenah to my father.

"Nice to see you again in less formal quarters, son," my father smiled, shaking his hand. "Thank you again for the help you gave Ana. I appreciate you looking out for her."

"Not a problem, sir. We're happy to back her up." Gawen's true meaning was clear. He'd helped me when they wouldn't and his next words drove his point home. "Not that she needed much. She's a force to be reckoned with."

"Yes," my father hummed. "I'm starting to see that."

I peeked at my father's aura and saw that it was even more open and loving at the moment than my mother's, something that surprised me. He's always been more guarded emotionally than she was, less demonstrative and more of a worrier when it came to our safety. Now, though, where her energy carried an angry edge, his seemed colored more by sadness, and maybe regret.

What I saw there spurred on my decision to lay out everything I knew. First, though, I knew I needed to start with an apology.

"Please, can everyone have a seat? I have something to say." My mom perched on the couch next to Hollis, forcing him closer to Jules, and my father took a seat next to her on the arm of the sofa. I stood up, pacing a bit as I waited for Gawen to sit back down. When he did, I faced them all.

"Mom, Dad, Hollis. I'm sorry, I want you all to know that. From the bottom of my heart, I really am." Tears welled in my eyes and my mother started to get up but I motioned for her to sit. I swiped the offending droplets from my eyes and went on. "I'm sorry, and know what I did was wrong, but maybe now you'll see that keeping me out of this isn't for the best. I know now that what happened to Khai is my fault. For a long time, I've been blaming you guys for keeping me in Aeden, for keeping me from going after what I love. I'll be honest. I was really,

really angry with you. All of you. Down in Valhalla, Khai and Airmed suffered for it. I didn't make it easy for either of them. But now I really get it. You were all trying to keep me safe." My father opened his mouth to speak, and I held up a hand. "You were right. But you were wrong, too. You needed me here. David needed me here. It wasn't the Light Guard or the Gregors who found the warpers. It was me."

"And look where that got us," Hollis grumbled. "My best friend taken, just so you could save that useless-"

"Hollis," my mother warned in a low voice. "Not now."

"No. It's okay. Hollis is right. Khai is in trouble and that is my fault. But he's my best friend, too. Which is why, whatever is happening next, I need to be on the front lines."

My father sprang up. "Are you out of your mind?"

"Alec." My mom tried to pull him back but he stalked out of reach.

"Don't you Alec me, Siri," he groused. "Our daughter here is ready to throw her life away, and she thinks I'm going to just-"

"Let her talk, Alec," my mom said. He crossed his arms over his chest, mirroring my own pose.

"Fine. Go ahead, Ana. You tell me why I shouldn't haul you back to Aeden right now."

He was only a couple feet away, looking down at me the same way he had the time I'd gone riding Ayita without telling anyone. Except now, I didn't quake in my boots, because I could see that it all came from a place of love. His aura was clear and pink, radiating desperate tendrils of concern towards my own.

"Because, I know something no one else knows. I've spoken with the local water elementals and they know something about what's happening. They've told me where there are more warpers nearby. They said there are fae there, too. It has to be Khai. It just has to."

Jules gasped and Hollis gripped her hand. "You didn't know?" he asked her, and she shook her head.

"I haven't told anyone," I said. "Just all of you."

"Where are they?" my father demanded.

I shook my head. "I can't tell you that. I don't care who comes along with me to save him, but I'll not be left behind again. And I'm sorry, but I just don't trust you not to do that if I tell you everything I know."

His face turned red and my mother rose to stand beside him.

"We understand," she said, gripping his hand tightly. "And we'll be there with you."

"Siri-"

"We will be there, with her," she repeated. "You can't keep her safe forever, Alec. She's right. This is her fight now."

"It's all our fight," Gawen said.

"You don't have to do that," I protested.

"No. But we will," Reenah said, shrugging gracefully. "It's what friends do."

My father sighed dramatically. "Fine. You're all crazy, but you're all adults. Legally, I can't tell you what to do. Ana, can you at least tell me how far this place is? What we're up against?"

"Not exactly. Water elementals experience the world in a really different way than we do. But I'm pretty sure we can get there in under an hour on foot. It's further upstream, along the river. That's all I can say. But I'd expect it's well fortified."

My father nodded. "Alright then. I will go and round up a team. Give me a few hours to prepare some back-up, at least."

"Yes, why don't we move out at midnight? That way, maybe most of their guards will be sleeping?" my mom said.

"And they'll have restricted night vision, unlike some of us," my dad said, kissing her on the nose. "I love the way you think."

"Blech," I said, pretending to vomit on the floor.

Mom ignored me and threw an arm around her husband, kissing him full on before disengaging and pushing him towards the door.

"Alright, move it. No time to lose," she said with a satisfied grin.

Gods, parents could be so mortifying.

I turned to Hollis, hoping to find some forgiveness there. He refused to look at me, storming out of the room behind my parents and slamming the door behind him.

"Well, that went well," I said, wringing my hands together. Jules jumped up and wrapped her arms around me.

"Don't pay any attention to him. He's just-"

"I know. And you know you're my best friend, too, right?"

"Well, duh. You can have more than one bestie."

"Just checking," I said, squeezing her tightly and letting go. "You guys, too. Gawen, Reenah? I haven't known you long, but I think you're both pretty amazing."

They both grinned back at me. "Like Jules said, duh," Gawen drawled.

"And what you guys said before, about coming with us-"

"Don't even try to talk us out of it," Reenah warned.

"I would never! But I did want to say thanks."

"Yeah, yeah, we know. Look, if we're heading out in a couple hours, I'm gonna need to catch some more Z's," Gawen said, stretching. "Don't leave without me?"

"Not in a million years," I vowed.

"Yeah, I'm gonna get some rest, too," Reenah seconded. "Maybe take a bath. Don't worry, bro, I'll set an alarm for us. See you ladies later."

"Perfecto," he said, throwing an arm around her and giving Jules and I salute as they left.

"What about you?" Jules asked after they had left.

"I think I'm going to see how David is settling in. I'm too wired to nap."

"Yeah, I hear you. But a bath sounds good. I'm right across from you guys, room 437. Reenah and Gawen are just down the hall in 448 and 50. In case you need us."

"Okay, 37, 48 and 50. Got it."

I followed her out into the hallway and we went our separate ways. Filled with nervous energy, I didn't bother taking the elevator. Instead, I climbed the stairs two at a time, my hands sweating with the nerves I'd been holding at bay. The confrontation with my parents and Hollis had shaken me, even though it had gone as well as could be expected. Outside David's room, I took a deep breath. This would be better. Seeing David was just what I needed.

I knocked lightly on the door and waited. I was about to knock again, when I heard a faint, "Come in."

"David, hi!" I smiled brightly, rushing to his side. He was still hooked up to some IV fluids and a machine to monitor his vitals. It irritated me, seeing the machines. His body wasn't broken. I'd healed that part of him, I was sure of it.

He tried to smile, but the lines of his mouth didn't line up right. In the end, it looked like a fallen soufflé – sad, deflated, but still holding some promise.

"How are you holding up? Are you feeling any better?" I pulled a chair over to his bed and sat down, holding his hand in mine.

"I guess. I don't know. No. Not really."

"Well, that's encouraging," I teased, trying to coax a real smile out of him. It didn't work.

"Yeah. I guess I'm all out of encouragement." David's voice was flat, dejected.

"That's okay. I have enough for the both of us. Optimism, too. You're going to be okay. It's just going to take some time." Noting that his hand still lay limp in mine, I rubbed it between my two palms trying to warm it up. Unbidden, the image of a dead fish I'd once found floating in our pond came back to me. The silver sunfish had felt the same when I'd picked it up, crying, to show my mother. David's energy was so low, even worse than hours before. I tried sending the warmth of Anansanna through to him, but it was like lighting a candle in a snowstorm.

Then, I realized he hadn't said anything.

"David?" I questioned. "Do you want to talk about it? What can I do to help? Whatever you need, I'm here for you."

"I know you are," he sighed. "Maybe that's part of the problem."

"What?" I didn't understand, and I felt like that cold front had just slapped me back with a gust of wind.

"You, being here. You're so, warm. Alive. I can't be what you want me to be. You want me to come back to you, I can feel it, but I can't. It's like, I'm empty inside. Hollow. Whatever powers I had? They're gone. Can you understand how that feels? All those emotions I used to feel, the colors I used to see around you, around everyone, they're gone. It's like I'm frozen inside. Broken."

"I know. I can feel it," I whispered. I started to tremble.

"I'm empty. Whatever I felt for you, it's gone, too."

"But, I saved you. Don't push me away now. At least give me some time." Part of me ached for him, but part of me was in shock, too.

"I just... I can't do this. Maybe someday my feelings will come back. Maybe someday I'll be healed, or even, not be healed, but just have a part of me that cares about anything. Right now, I can't. Look at me, Ana."

I raised my eyes from where I'd been staring at our hands, still joined. Fire and ice. I stared into his eyes. They'd always seemed so warm to me, but now, they were just brown. Flat. He pulled his hand from mine.

"I'm breaking your heart, and I can't even bring myself to care. I should be sorry, but I'm not sure I even know what that means anymore."

I pushed my fist against my lips, choking back a sob. My body started to shake, but I refused to cry. I almost wished he had been mind-warped. That there was something there to stare back at me, rather than this empty husk of a man I'd loved. Because I had loved him and he had loved me. Hadn't he? Somehow, I found myself at the door, one hand on the knob. I couldn't even remember standing. I turned one last time and stared at him, searching for something, anything, even the tiniest sign that the David I knew was still in there.

I found nothing. His aura was dim, as dark as the cloud of sadness threatening to overtake me. Still, I knew it wasn't his fault. The warpers had done something to him. Maybe it could be fixed, and maybe it couldn't. But it wasn't his fault. The warpers hadn't just destroyed the man I loved, they'd stolen away any justification I could have had to be angry at his words. All that was left to me was raw pain, the gaping wound where our love had wrenched itself free.

"It's okay, David. I understand. I felt it when I saved you. Something is broken inside you, and I wish I could help you fix it, but I don't know how." I paused. "Friends?"

His body slumped, relaxing into the pillow. His lips curved into an almost smile.

"There you go, saving me again. This time from myself."

"It's what I do, I guess." I smiled back at him, glossing over my true emotions. I thought I might throw up.

He nodded.

"Friends, then. If I can remember how to do that, even."

"That's okay. You're doing just fine," I said gently. "Is it okay if I check in on you again soon?"

"Yes, of course."

"Good. Get some rest."

"You, too," he said sleepily. I started to leave the room. "Oh, and Ana?"

"Yes, David?"

"Thanks again. You know, for saving me."

"I wasn't alone."

"I know what you did. Thank you."

"Okay. Goodnight, David."

I watched his lids close, and closed the door as quietly as I could.

Somehow, I'd lost him again. But not entirely. He was still in there somewhere, I'd caught a glimpse of it for a moment. I supposed a live, broken friend was infinitely better than a dead, distant boyfriend. It had to be. So what if my entire heart felt like it was breaking into a million tiny pieces?

Giving in to moment, I slid down the cold cement wall of the stairwell and allowed my heart to spill over, tears running down my face as I let the sobs come.

Chapter 8

Dressed mostly in black, walking the trail along the river, our group got some odd looks from the few midnight joggers we encountered. One woman, a small leashed corgi in tow, gave us as wide a berth as she could. I couldn't blame her. Despite the promise to her husband to stay out of the fray, Callie had decided to join us, bringing along her own special ops starseeds. The team of six didn't introduce themselves or say much of anything, and I felt relieved not to have to engage in extra conversation. I was used to the serious demeanor of Light Guards, but these guys took it to a whole new level.

No one smiled or spoke. Between the starseeds and my friends and family, our procession varied wildly in age: from me at nineteen to Callie in what I gauged to be her early sixties. Glancing at the weathered woman walking beside Callie, pistols strapped to her thighs, I wondered how much of it had to do with the Flare. Or, rather, the lack of it. Is this what most people had been like before the flare? Harder? Heavier? Their energy felt dense, and I could sense the difference in their cells from the rest of humanity. They weren't immortal, and they never would be. Not even close.

Somehow, I found that comforting. Their lifespan shorter, healing capacity diminished, surely the starseeds would do everything they could to stay healthy. Stay out of harm's way. Hopefully, they would spare the same attention for the rest of the team.

I could heal tissue, repair bones, but I couldn't bring back the dead.

Trying not to think about it, I stared at the sky. The night was dark, the barest sliver of moon hanging like a lopsided frown over the horizon. I refused to think of it as any sort of sign. Of course, the heavens weren't angry with us. No. I had to stop being silly. It was a beautiful night, and the fact that it was so dark was a blessing, surely, more than anything else.

I tore my eyes away from the sky and scanned the buildings coming up. We'd emerged from the wilds of the park, the trail bringing us to a more congested, settled area. Suddenly, instead of marsh grasses and trees, there were boathouses and mansions, warehouses and high-rises.

How would we know where the warpers were hiding?

I thought back to what the elementals had told me. A large building with walls like water. Rainbow walls. Iridescent? Again, I looked at the sky. I knew some glass was treated to reflect the light in a dazzling prismatic display, but at night the walls would be dim, probably black like the surface of the Charles.

The closest buildings were made of brick and concrete. One was sided with deep chestnut wood planks. I squinted ahead. Around the corner, I spied a building that seemed to fit the faerie description. Big. Shiny. In the night, it was dark, but the barely-there moon reflected in its surface like Venus on parade, sparkling and iridescent.

Excited, I picked up my pace. Did the building have a dock? Was this it?

Two boats were moored, the space for a third empty.

Three large boats at rest, the water faerie had said. This had to be it. And the heavens had blessed us, for it appeared at least some of the warpers were out enjoying a midnight cruise.

"That's it," I said, stopping in my tracks and pointing at the building. We were still a good fifty yards away. Because of the way the trail wound along the river, from here we could only see the back of the building, not the front. Part of the structure rested right above the water, with large doors for securing more boats inside. The doors glimmered, though they appeared to be made of heavily fortified steel, not glass.

"Are you sure?" my father asked. "It doesn't look particularly well-defended."

"Appearances can be deceiving," Callie said grimly. "There are warpers inside, I can hear them. Four, at least. And more. Starseeds, or maybe fae, I don't know. Whoever they are, they're not happy."

"The elementals said we'd find fae here, unhappy fae. It's got to be Khai. Do you sense him?" I asked.

Callie scrunched up her face in apology. "Sorry, I can't say. There are men; women, too. But I can't tell who they are just from their thoughts. It doesn't work like that."

"I know a way to find out," Hollis growled. He moved, ready to strike, and my father grabbed his arm.

"Wait. Not you." He motioned to the team at Callie's side. "You first. Assess the situation and secure the perimeter."

The weathered woman looked at Callie, who nodded, and then they were gone, black figures disappearing into the night.

We waited, seconds ticking by.

"Six cameras. Two guards at the street," Callie said, a faraway look in her eyes.

"How can you tell?" Hollis asked.

"Unagi." She tapped her forehead. I had no idea what that word meant, but I knew she must be communicating with her team telepathically.

"She's a reader," I told Hollis, who still looked confused.

"Oh. Why didn't she just say so?"

"Kids." My mom rolled her eyes and Callie laughed. Then, her face sobered.

"Cameras offline. Guards disabled. We're a go. My team will stay outside."

"Make sure they watch the dock, too. The elementals told me there are usually three boats, not two."

Callie nodded. Her eyes lost focus again, and then cleared. "It's done. Everybody ready?"

"Oh sure, we live for this sort of thing."

Gawen's off-hand remark earned him a sharp glance from my father, and he flushed.

"Sorry, Mr. Ward."

"This is serious, Gawen. Stay focused."

"Yessir. Of course."

My father took point, jogging toward the house, Hollis and my mom right on his heels. Gawen grabbed my hand, giving it a squeeze, and we followed, Reenah on his other side, with Callie bringing up the rear. We made our way up the front stairs as a group, careful not to make any noise. At the door, the building seemed smaller, only two stories above the boat storage area, not much larger than a big house. There were no obvious windows, though I assumed portions of the glass allowed one to look outside from within. Outside, I couldn't see a thing. What was it with starseeds and their spooky glass buildings? I liked shiny things as much as the next girl, but honestly.

Behind me, Callie snickered. "I never thought of it that way. I have a thing for shiny things, too, but I never thought it had something to do with being a starseed. Interesting."

"What?" my dad asked.

"Nothing," Callie and I answered in unison.

"Now what? Do we just knock?" Gawen asked.

"Allow me." My father shouldered past us, then shocked me by opening the door quickly and efficiently with a set of lock picks. Seriously? Who was this guy? I'd always thought of him, a former Light Guard, standing guard over the portals of Aeden, maybe engaging in some hand-to-hand combat. I knew he'd seen some fierce battles, been a hero many times over. I'd never imagined that he had trod on the wrong side of the law to do it.

"I love it when you do that," my mom said, watching him with admiration.

"If you like that, I'd be happy to show you what I did to the cameras." One of Callie's men grinned at her, his teeth flashing against his dark skin in the night.

She laughed quietly and my father raised an eyebrow. "No time for flirting, Siri. Let's move."

"Spoilsport," she grinned, hip-checking my dad. They'd always been warm and easy with each other, more like kids in love than regular parents. On archeological digs, it got worse, their institutional enthusiasm carrying over into their own relationship. This was the first time I'd been on a dangerous mission with them, though, and I saw how it lit them up. They were enjoying this, I realized with a bit of shock. My father's eyes were glowing more brilliantly than I'd ever seen, and I could tell it wasn't just the adrenaline of a risky situation.

It was too gross to bear thinking about.

Feeling a bit dazed as we headed inside, I scoped out the area for potential hazards, trying to sense Khai as I went.

Nothing. Well, nothing good, anyway.

I could sense some warper energy signatures several rooms away. It wasn't hard to tell what they were. Their auras were cold, dark. The energy around them twisted in on itself in an ugly tangle, lashing out occasionally like whips. No wonder few starseed travelers became warpers. Anyone who could see their energy would be turned off. Who would want to become *that*?

I tapped my dad on the shoulder and motioned down the hall with my head, holding up three fingers. His eyes narrowed and he gestured for my friends and me to stay where we were. Not missing a beat, my mother was already striding down the hall, followed closely by Hollis.

Using my auric sight, I watched the fight unfold. Dark energy swirled to meet auras of varying color and brightness. It looked like a vicious fight, but I wasn't worried. I knew we would prevail. My parents were too emotionally invested and battle-hardened for it to go any other way. For them, fighting had always been a dance, easy as breathing. I could hold my own, but I knew I would just get in the way this time. Instead, itching to help, I started prowling the empty rooms. The warpers were here. The elementals had said we'd find fae here, too. So where were they? Where were Khai, Cliff and the others?

We found the stairs to the boat storage area below, but there was nothing there to indicate any sort of basement facility like the one we'd found in Salem.

"Damn it," Jules said, sounding as frustrated as I felt. "Where are they?"

I shook my head, not having an answer. We'd searched every room in the place. There was nothing. Maybe there was something in with the warpers? We found everyone else in a comfy game room, the warpers unconscious and trussed up like turkeys on the floor. A line of security monitors broadcasted fields of snow, but the guards seemed to have been watching a soccer game on TV instead of doing their job. I was glad no one on our team seemed hurt, other than a few bruised faces, but I couldn't help feeling deflated. With the warpers unconscious, we couldn't even question them.

"Everybody, move out. We need to search this place top to bottom," Dad said.

"We already did, Mr. Ward," Gawen answered. There's nothing here."

"But that can't be." My mom's eyes widened. "If there's nothing here, why have so many guards?"

No one seemed to have an answer for that. Something was bothering me though. We'd missed something, we all knew it. But what?

Then I remembered. Outside, it had been clear that there was an upper story to the building. So where were the stairs?

"We've missed something. The stairs!" I exclaimed. "Everybody, look for a hidden staircase. There's another floor above us, there has to be a way to get up there."

Immediately, everyone fanned out, testing doors, knocking on walls. In the end, it was Hollis who found it – a false wall inside a shower stall on the first floor.

"The boot prints inside were a dead giveaway. I mean, who wears shoes in the shower?" he asked, shrugging.

"Well done," my father said, clapping him on the back. The entrance was narrow; the stairs, steep and dark. I couldn't sense anything above us, but I had to hope. One by one, we climbed upwards. As we moved, I felt something eating away at my energy, like my soul was being sucked out slowly.

In Salem, I hadn't noticed, but this time I recognized the feeling for what it was.

"Careful," I said in a low voice as I emerged onto the second floor. "This place is lined with the same material that blocks the light of Anansanna. It'll sap our powers."

"That's not possible," my mom protested.

"Really? Then what the hell do you think really happened to us back in Salem? You think I just made all that up before? Stay here too long, and you'll be just like any other human."

My mother blanched.

"Ana, I didn't mean-"

"Save it." I held up a hand. "Just help me find Khai." Already, the others were checking out rooms along the hallway, each of them empty.

"Over here," Callie said, pointing at a closed door. "There are people in here."

"Fae?"

"I don't know. Maybe. Their auras are weak, almost nonexistent. I couldn't sense them until I got close. And..."

"What?" I said, pushing her out of the way. I reached out with my inner vision and looked for myself. "They're not moving," I whispered, opening the door at the same time.

"Ana, wait," my father protested, rushing towards me, but of course I didn't listen. I had to see for myself.

Nothing prepared me for what I found. I was expecting something horrific: dying fae, Khai covered with wounds. What I saw was so much worse.

Plain wooden rockers, all in a row, facing a holo-wall. You could see the river outside, daytime footage reproduced in gritty, low-color pixels. The tech was old. Shoddy. It had to be intentional, a way of mocking the viewers. Like, *see, here? This is what you're missing.*

I felt sick.

One of the rockers creaked, a solitary swaying, and my eyes took in the occupants. Even from the back, I could tell Khai was not here. These people all had heads of hair in varying stages of grey. Whoever they were, they'd been here longer than a couple of days.

My hand went to my mouth, taking it all in. How could the warpers do this, to anyone? Fae or human, what had these people done to deserve imprisonment?

My lips tightened into a firm line.

Nothing. They'd done nothing. No one could ever deserve to have their life-force slowly drained, their soul sucked away. I didn't care who they were, what they did. It was too cruel. These people, their auras were so weak, it was a miracle they were even alive. I wondered what else the warpers had done to them, what their aim was. Everyone crowded into the room, rushing to the elderly viewers, taking pulses, helping them up.

"It's okay," my mom said to one of them, supporting the woman with an arm around her waist. "My name is Siri. We're here to take you home."

"Home?" the woman echoed.

"It's a trick!" one of the men wailed weakly, backing away from two of Callie's men.

"No, it's not. We're here to rescue you." I flew forward and clasped his hand, channeling as much healing energy as I could into him. If he was fae, my touch should bring automatic comfort, a bonus all fae experienced from being so connected to the light. He tried to pull away, but I held on tight. "Please, let us help you."

He shook his head. "No, it's another trick. Don't listen to them. Mara, resist!"

"Mara?" Reenah said, looking away from the man she'd been helping up. She looked at me, then the man, and jerked backward in shock. "Oh my gods, it can't be-"

Gawen glanced up at her. In a flash, he was at Reenah's side, helping her stand. She barely noticed, her eyes fixed on the man next to me. Her mouth worked, slowly, like she had to remember how to speak. Finally, one word broke through, forced out on shaking breath.

"Dad?"

Chapter 9

Time seemed to speed up after that. Reenah's mother and father, Mara and Tae, made an effort to move more quickly, embracing a daughter they hadn't seen in almost a decade. Watching them, I think almost everyone in the room had tears in their eyes. Still, there was no time to linger.

"Transport is on the way, ETA two minutes," Callie said. "Let's get these people downstairs and back to safety."

"The guards?" I asked.

"My team is already on it. The warpers are still out of commission, but I have plenty of questions for them when they're ready to talk."

"You think they'll talk?" my dad mused.

"Oh, I know they will," Callie said darkly. "You just leave them to me, Alec."

By the time we'd herded Reenah's parents and the others downstairs, a large tour bus had pulled up and was idling outside with its doors open. Callie's team flanked the vehicle.

"The warpers?" Callie asked.

"Secured below," one of the men said, smirking as he nodded towards a locked luggage bin by the rear wheels.

"Perfect," she purred. She turned and clapped her hands briskly. "Come on, all aboard. I know everybody has lots of questions, and I promise, we'll get everything sorted out at headquarters after some hot baths, warm meals, and calls to your families. Come on, that's it." She helped a white-haired man limp up the stairs into the bus, patting him on the back. "Everything is going to be okay, I promise. You're safe now."

"Is it true? Are we really saved?" Mara looked at her husband with bleary eyes. She seemed dazed. Lost. "After all these years, has someone found us?"

"Yes, sweetness, they have." Tae kissed the silvery hair above her temple, looking at me gratefully. "This is really happening, right? We're not dreaming it? I've dreamed of going home so many times."

"No, Dad, it's not a dream. We're really here." Reenah's voice hitched as she rubbed his shoulder, steering him towards the bus.

The ride back to HQ was quick and quiet. I think everyone was too overwhelmed with what we'd found to talk yet. We were too busy processing. At least, I know I was. When we got back, Callie assigned an operative to each of the other rescued fae, instructing them to help them to their rooms and do whatever they could to help them feel comfortable. Free.

I knew her heart was in the right place, but I was pretty sure it would take a lot more than a night of comfort to heal their hearts and minds. They needed to go home, find their families. Healing like this could only come from within, and it would take time. Lots and lots of time.

Unfortunately, time was the one thing we didn't have.

I watched Reenah guiding her mother towards the elevator, Gawen and her father trailing behind them. Mara moved listlessly like she didn't really believe she had anywhere good to go to. Like she didn't really believe her daughter was holding her by the arm. Her aura wasn't just weak; it was thin, like mist. One strong wind and she might just dissolve into nothingness. Somehow, she'd been holding on by a thread for the gods knew how long. I prayed, for Reenah's sake, that we weren't too late – that Mara's aura could be rewoven, from thread to twine to the strongest webbing.

Reenah led Mara into the lift, but Tae pulled back, saying something to Gawen. I watched as the doors closed on Reenah and her mother, and Gawen helped Tae walk back to us.

"What is it?" Callie asked, grasping both Tae's hands in hers. "What can we do for you?"

"It's not what you can do for me. It's what I can do for you. The warpers who took us, they rarely spoke to us, barely treated us like people. They acted like we were animals, lab rats beneath their notice."

"It's okay Mr. Shin. We can talk about what they did to you later," Gawen said gently. "Right now, you should rest."

"Rest? I've had years to rest," Tae spat. "Gods forbid that what happened to us should befall any other fae. That's what I want to talk to you about." His dark eyes burned into mine, then Callie's. "The warpers, they didn't think I was able-minded enough to pay attention to them anymore. But when they talked, I always listened. I hoped, prayed, that one day- Well, that day finally came. You came. Thank you, and thank the gods."

I grasped his hands in mine, gripping them tightly. "What did you hear, Mr. Shin? What can you tell us?"

"Our guards were celebrating last night, excited that they might finally get promoted and moved to another facility. They'd heard there was a break-in at a larger

63

research center, and everyone was being evacuated to another location. They seemed to think that we would be moving soon, too. The men teased us, said that we'd be seeing more of our own kind soon, for all the good it would do us."

"Do you know where they were taking you? Anything you can tell us, please." I drifted off, staring into his eyes. Hungry for information. Yearning to find Khai.

Reenah's father nodded. "Yes, of course. I-" He shuddered, sinking into Gawen. "I guess I do need to rest. All this excitement…"

"Here, Mr. Shin, let me help you sit." Gawen led Tae over to a group of chairs by the wall.

"Do you know what he's going to tell us?" I whispered to Callie as we followed.

"No," she said, frowning. "I can't read him. All fae are harder for me to read. Except you," she grinned. "You're still broadcasting loud and clear."

"Sorry," I mumbled, trying to put my shields back in place. "Better?"

"Better. Most starseeds wouldn't hear a whisper now. Of course, I'm not most starseeds." She winked at me and then sat across from Tae Shin. "Mr. Shin, I think you should know, the warpers have indeed taken more fae. One young man was lost just the other day. We had hoped to find all of you under one roof, but it seems the trail ends with you."

Tae slumped into his chair. "The warpers thought we were too far gone. Too aged and feeble to care or hear anything. But I heard. I always heard." He licked his lips, wetting them. "They have a large research center in Connecticut, deep in the woods of the northwest corner. A place with a woman's name. Sandra? Susan? It began with an S, I'm sure of it." He exhaled and ran a shaky hand over his face. "I am sorry I cannot be of more help."

"It's another piece of the puzzle. Thank you." Callie stood and shook Tae's hand. "Now I know where to start with the men we have in custody."

"They won't tell you anything," Tae trembled. "They have no conscience."

"You leave them to me," Callie said, patting him on the shoulder. "Gawen, Ana, please show Tae to his room. You all could use some rest." She paused. "Why did they have you up so late in that room, anyway? It was after midnight when we found you. You should have been tucked into beds, sleeping."

Tae shrugged. "Another experiment. They were trying to disrupt our circadian rhythms, see if they could speed our aging process even further."

"Why?" Gawen asked, sounding shocked.

"Why did the men who took us do anything they did? I don't know. They never shared their reasoning with us, only their hatred. Maybe that was the only reason they had."

Something stabbed me in the chest, hearing that. Fear? Despair? I wasn't sure, but I decided to go with empathy. The days and years he'd suffered at the warpers hands: I couldn't let that happen to anyone else. This wasn't just about Khai or Cliff. In that moment, I knew I'd sacrifice myself if it would prevent even one more person being subjected to their experiments.

"Let's hope not," Callie said, looking at me. Gawen and Tae took her reply at face value, but I knew she was talking to me. That she had heard my thoughts, again.

I pasted an innocent smile on my face, pretending I had no idea what she was talking about, and reached out to help Tae stand.

Callie stalked off, presumably heading for whatever made do as their dungeon around here, and Gawen took Tae's other arm. Between the two of us, we were able to half-carry, half-steer Reenah's father towards the elevator. Once there, I wasn't sure what button to press.

"Where did they take everybody else?" I asked.

"I don't know. Let's see if Reenah's back in her room." Gawen said.

She was. She opened the door quickly at our light knock, as if she'd been waiting for us. Laying a finger on her lips, she beckoned us inside.

"She wouldn't leave me," she whispered, gesturing towards the bed where her mother lay sleeping, curled into a tight fetal curl. "But she kept asking for you." Reenah looked at her father, tears in her eyes.

He placed a hand against her cheek and pressed his forehead against hers. Then inhaled deeply, like he was drawing her in. "I missed you," he said simply.

She sobbed, once, and threw her arms around him. She hugged him so tightly, I feared he might break, but I didn't say a word. This needed to happen. They needed to be with each other. I watched Reenah lead her father to the bed, where he curled around his wife. Reenah climbed into bed behind him, lying on her side, one hand resting on her father's shoulder. I looked at Gawen, and he nodded, pressing his lips together. It was time to go. We all needed rest.

Back in my own room, I turned up the far-infrared heating system and lay on the bed fully clothed, hoping the warm, invisible rays of light would lull me to sleep.

It didn't work.

My mind was a hotbed of fretful ideas and dead-end plans. Just when I thought I'd run out of things to think about, Khai would pop into my head. Khai, wrestled to the ground, arms strung up between several thugs. Khai, trying to call up lightning, and failing. Yelling at me to run. And Khai, on the Long Trail, all those weeks ago. So happy when he'd realized I was a water fae, figuring it out even before I did, and then so angry because he suspected David wasn't who he seemed to be. I remembered how we'd fought, how I'd stormed off with David and Jules. If I had just come clean then, if I had just told him and Hollis everything, maybe none of this would have happened.

But that wouldn't be right, would it? Reenah wouldn't have found her parents. I wouldn't have met Callie, wouldn't have been part of taking down the warpers.

And that, I realized, would have been a tragedy. Because this wasn't just personal now, I realized. It was about what was right. I was a healer, at heart. And so many people needed healing, people I hadn't even met yet. People that needed saving. My father had raised me to be like him, too. To save people. I thought it had just been for his peace of mind, but now I could see that it was for my own, too.

I needed to do this. To save Khai. To help the starseeds. College could wait. Airmed could wait. This was life – sometimes you had to learn on the job.

Feeling warm and more at ease than I had in while, I closed my eyes and let myself sink into the dreamtime.

Chapter 10

I dreamed of sunshine, red and gold; of dark cathedral pines and the forests of home. I did not see David, or Phineas, or anything reeking of warpers. Gleaming white beneath the trees, I saw only Ayita.

My young fleet waited patiently for me to approach, her massive green eyes shimmering with emotion as she ducked her muzzle towards my outstretched hand.

"I've missed you, girl." As it had been all my life, I could not hear her thoughts. I never would, not now. I wasn't an earth fae, and never would be. But I could feel her emotions, how her heart leapt at my presence.

Was she really here? Were we really connecting in the dreamtime, as I had with David, or was she simply a figment of my imagination?

I decided I didn't care. We were here, dream or not, together for the first time in months, and we would do what came naturally.

We would ride.

I gripped the long silvery threads of her mane and swung myself up onto her naked back. We'd never used a saddle, and wouldn't need one now. I settled in, centering my hips above her spine, took a deep breath and smiled.

"Fly, Ayita. Fly!" I shouted the last, and we were off, Ayita's hooves thundering dully on the dense forest floor.

Swiftly, we climbed through the woods, leaping over stream beds and fallen trees. There was no obstacle too great for Ayita. Her kind was the stuff of legend, the unicorns of old. They could leap 40-foot chasms: the woods of the Northeast held few such impassable barriers.

I didn't think; I didn't speak. I just flew. Finally, at the top of a mountain, Ayita stood. We were above the tree line, overlooking valleys from our perch of bare rock, standing high where the mountain had been scalped by glaciers thousands of years before. I slid off Ayita's back and grabbed a handful of moss, using it to gently scrub down her damp coat. As my hands ran over her, I allowed memories of what had happened to flow through my head, telling Ayita everything. Because even though I couldn't hear her thoughts, I knew she could hear mine. We'd always been close, as one, despite the language barrier. Fleet bonded with their riders for life, and Ayita was mine, all mine. I'd been riding her for almost as long as I'd been walking. While I told her my story using words and thoughts, she huffed and shifted nervously, stamping her foot and tossing her head when I told her about Khai's capture. She'd always had a soft spot for Khai, allowing him to ride behind me when Hollis' fleet would not.

Again, I wondered if she was really here. Did fleets dream? Tired, I set down the moss and sat down on the bare stone, Ayita collapsing beside me neatly. Whatever this was, wherever we were, I was weary. I closed my eyes and nestled into Ayita's neck, allowing myself to just stop thinking.

A knock at the door roused me. Alone and in bed, Ayita was gone. Feeling empty, I padded to the door and Gawen barged in.

"They're leaving," he said, grim-faced.

"Who?" I asked, barely functioning yet.

"The Shins. Reenah's taking them back to Aeden. To their home." He said the last word strangely, as if it left a bitter taste in his mouth.

"Um, okay. Should we go say goodbye?"

"Why do you think I'm here?" he grumbled. "Reenah asked for you. There are some people here, they want to talk to you, too."

"Really? Who?" I warbled from the bathroom, speaking around the sonic toothbrush in my mouth.

"Khai's parents. They got here last night."

My heart skipped a beat and I tried to ignore it, spitting into the sink and rinsing out my mouth.

"Claire and Brenin are here?" I asked nervously, pulling on some clean clothes, barely sparing my choices a glance as I drew them from my bag. I ran my fingers through my hair. I probably should have washed up more, but with the Mirros waiting... I needed to see them, try to explain. Claire and Brenin were like my aunt and uncle. They had to understand. Right?

I shook my head, pinning back a piece of hair over one ear, trying to tame some of the crazy red curls swirling around my face.

They would never understand.

How could they, when even I didn't?

Exhaling forcefully, I left the bathroom, almost colliding with Gawen.

"Okay. I'm ready. Let's go."

"Everybody is in the dining hall waiting," he said. Anger was simmering just under his voice, but it barely registered, simply adding a sort of dissonant white noise under the mist of my own nervousness. We rode the

70

elevator in silence and he followed me to the cafeteria. Scared, I grabbed his hand without thinking, but that only added to my unease, his own emotions bubbling through me more strongly now.

"What's your problem?" I asked more rudely than I meant to, snatching my hand away.

"Who says I have a problem?" he replied snottily.

I opened my mouth to say something I would probably regret, but closed it when I felt a tap on my shoulder.

"Ana? Oh, by the gods, Ana!" Claire's gentle arms spun me and drew me into a warm embrace. I stood there, not moving, shocked that my mother's oldest friend wasn't screaming into my face. And then her husband Brenin was hugging us both, his youthful energy so much like Khai's that I found myself bursting into tears and clinging to them both like a baby howler monkey.

"I couldn't save him," I sobbed against Claire's shoulder."

"Shh, baby, it's okay. We know. It's not your fault." She patted me and we came apart. I protested, wiping my face.

"But I could have-"

"Don't, please. Siri's told us everything. There's nothing you could have done," she said.

"Nor should have done," Brenin declared, looking down at me with his clear blue eyes. Darker than Khai, his skin gleamed mahogany under the fluorescent lights. "Now, at least, we have a chance to get him back. Without you, we might have lost you both. Lost everyone."

"Yeah, and Reenah never would have gotten her parents back," Gawen said. I noticed he didn't sound too happy about that, and again wondered what his problem was.

"I guess." I shrugged. Behind Brenin, I saw Reenah waving us over happily. "Should we eat? I mean, are you-"

"We've eaten. Your parents already ordered for you, come, sit down." Claire took me by the hand and I could feel that everything they'd said was true. By some miracle, she really didn't blame me. She felt...hopeful. Not happy, but okay. She was doing okay.

"How can you be smiling?" I asked her. Her skin was paler than usual. It had already lost the gleam of summer, and she had dark circles under her eyes.

"I'm smiling because you are like a daughter to me, and you're here. Alive. I just know that everything is going to turn out. If your mom says she will bring Khai back, then I know she will. Siri is an amazing woman. You're an amazing woman. If anyone can find Khai, it's the two of you."

"Not Hollis or my dad?" I blurted without thinking. I couldn't believe she was lumping me in with my mother's power of amazingness.

"Psht. Boys. We know who holds the real power, don't we?" We giggled conspiratorially and sat down side by side at the table like schoolgirls.

Just as Claire had said, my parents had ordered breakfast for me already – a large bowl of fresh strawberries heaped with whipped almond cream and drizzled with honey, one of my favorite combinations. A tall glass of fresh orange juice sat nearby, along with a chocolate muffin. Of course. My mother could never resist anything chocolate on a menu. Like mother like daughter. A plate of eggs and toast sat in front of an empty seat by Reenah, and Gawen sat down. He must have placed his order before he'd come to get me. I sat down across from him at the large round table and took a slow sip of juice, glancing around as I did so. Mara was leaning against Tae, but her eyes looked clearer, more sentient. Reenah sat on her other side, holding her hand tightly, like Mara was a bird that might flit away and disappear. Gawen wasn't looking at any of the Shins. A casual observer would have thought he was too busy shoveling food into his mouth, but I knew better. His aura was compressed, drawn in and shielded. Whatever he was feeling, thinking, he didn't want anyone to know.

The mystery of it only strengthened my desire to get into his head. I popped a strawberry into my mouth, considering. Should I try to break through his auric shields, see what I could sense? It would be an invasion of privacy, but it would also be good practice for dealing with warpers, I was sure. Still... it wouldn't be right. Frowning to myself, I discarded the idea. If Gawen wanted to talk, he would. Instead of breaking his trust, I dedicated my attention to devouring the delectable breakfast before me. I'd just filled my mouth with a fresh spoonful of cream when my father cleared his throat.

"As most of you know, the Shins will be returning to Aeden this morning with their daughter and the other rescued fae from the boathouse. We believe a familiar environment, combined with the cutting-edge medicine of Valhalla's Fourth Tower, will be of the most benefit to their recovery."

"You believe they can recover?" I asked, surprised.

"We hope so, yes. Their minds, at least, if not their bodies. Anansanna remains a mystery to us in many ways. Who knows what benefit her direct proximity may have upon their systems?"

"Good. At least you have a plan," I said. My father peered at me suspiciously, as if suspecting I was mocking him, but I wasn't.

I meant it. Plans were good. I'd gone off half-cocked enough times to know the damage a lack of planning could impose.

"Right, well. Claire, Brenin. Now that you've had some time to think about it, what would you like to do? Do you want to come with us, or wait in Aeden with the others? As I explained earlier, we don't have a clear idea of what we'll be facing on mission."

"We will wait in Aeden," Claire said, her husband's arm coming around her for support. We're not fighters, either of us. We'd only get in the way."

Brenin stroked his goatee, more somber than I'd ever seen him. "We'll make sure everything is ready for Khai's return. You know, Alec, I wasn't happy with you when you recommended Khai for duty with the Guard. I didn't raise my son to be a warrior. The last words we had between us weren't easy. I need to make sure he knows that I support him, whatever he's doing. I can't have our last conversation be the end of things between us." He winced. "I guess, what I'm trying to say is that we're trusting you— I'm trusting you—to bring our boy back to us in one piece. To make this right."

"You have my word, Brenin, whatever we can do..." My father trailed off, fine speeches not being his thing.

"Alec and Siri are unstoppable, you know that," Claire said, directing a wobbly smile up at her husband. "They can do this."

"Of course we can," my mom said, beaming across the table at her friend. "I saved the world, remember? What're a few aliens to a girl like me?"

I snorted. "You better not let Callie hear you say that. I think she could probably give you a run for your money. Where is she, anyway?"

"Questioning the prisoners," my mom said airily. "Last I heard, one of them cracked at dawn. Now she's trying to confirm the intel by putting pressure on the others."

"Pressure? Why doesn't she just mind-warp them?" Hollis asked. "She's a speaker, right? Can't she just order them to tell her?"

My mom frowned at him. "Maybe she thinks doing things like a warper is dangerous. As well you should know. I've told you enough about the days of the Dark for you to understand-"

"Yeah, yeah," Hollis drawled, interrupting. "The Shades were bad news. We know. But so are these guys. We don't know what they're doing to Khai right now, how long he can wait. What if-"

I cut him off, not wanting to hear the gruesome what ifs he might have imagined. "You can't always mind-warp someone, Hollis. Callie told me. There are ways to resist speakers and readers. Plus, look around. You can see the damage messing with a person's mind can do. You really want to be a part of that?"

Hollis glared at me. "Better that than lose my best friend, yeah. I think I'm okay with that."

"Hollis!" my father barked. "That's enough. Sounds like you need to work some of that anger off. Come on." My dad pushed his chair back and stood up. "How about you, Ana, Siri?"

"Why, I'd love to work up a sweat with you, Alec, I thought you'd never ask," my mother grinned and took his hand.

After pretending to puke on the floor, I laughed. "I'm good, thanks."

Jules stood. She'd been so quiet during the meal, I'd hardly noticed she was there.

"I'd like to come, Mrs. A, if you don't mind. Ana taught me some things over the summer, but I'd love to learn a few new moves."

Hollis muttered something under his breath and stalked away.

"Don't mind him. He's just worried." My mother leaned down to kiss Claire and Brenin on the cheek, telling them she'd see them soon, then linked arms with Jules and my father. They turned and left, following my brother at a leisurely pace.

"It's just us then. Gawen, Ana, will you see us off?" Claire glanced at her watch. "We're supposed to be meeting in the lobby in ten minutes. The starseeds have arranged a transport and some guards to accompany us to Aeden, as well as two of their own medical team."

"You're leaving already?" I asked and she nodded. "Well, then of course, Claire, I wouldn't want to be anywhere else. Gawen?"

"Yeah, sure," he said dully.

Reenah squinted at him, as if noticing for the first time that he wasn't quite himself. "Gawen, I haven't had a chance to talk to our paren- I mean, your parents. Do you think you could call them? Tell them what's happened? We'll need them to ship everything of Mom and Dad's from storage down to Valhalla." Reenah's words tripped over themselves as she gushed. I couldn't begin to imagine how elated she must be to have her parents back. "I think it will really help for them to have all our old stuff around, you know, to remind them. My stuff, too, I guess."

Gawen's head whipped up. "You're moving out?"

"Well, yeah, I won't be needing my room anymore. I'll be living with my parents now." She looked at him like he was braindead.

"But, what about school?" Gawen sounded panicked, which was odd, considering he'd never struck me as the overly studious type.

"Oh, no, I'm not moving out of our apartment!" Reenah covered her mouth and tittered, while Gawen gawked at her. I knew she was on an emotional high, but could she really not see how agitated he was? "I'll be back at school in a few weeks, I hope. But I don't need to keep taking up space at your parent's house. Not anymore."

"Is that what you think? That you were taking up space?" Gawen's voice was hollow.

"Well, I-"

"Dammit, Reenah, you were family." He scowled and pushed away from the table. "You know what? You can see yourself off. I'm gonna go train with Jules."

"But, Gawen, I-" Reenah looked up at him, confused.

"We'll send your stuff as soon as I can, don't give it another thought," he said, waving over his shoulder as he walked away without sparing her another glance.

"What's his deal?" she grumbled. "Isn't he happy for me?"

"I'm sure he is, it's just..."

"What?"

"I think you hurt his feelings. You're like his sister, you know? And now you're leaving."

"Yeah, I guess. But it's not like I'm not coming back to school. I just need to spend a couple of weeks getting my parents settled in down below. And you guys are going to be busy, anyway, doing all this stuff." She waved her hand around at the room full of starseed diners.

"Yeah. He'll be fine. Don't worry, okay? I'll keep an eye on him." If there was one thing I could be sure of, it was that if it came down to it, I would be the one getting captured, never one of my friends. Never again.

"Promise?"

"You bet. Actually, I'll make you a deal – I'll cheer up Gawen, and you can give Airmed a message from me." I linked arms with Reenah and walked her towards the lobby, crafting an apology to the Ancient herbalist as I went.

Chapter 11

After securing Claire's promise to look after Reenah, and Reenah's promise to charm Airmed into forgiving me, I decided to join my family in the training arena. The idea of planting one on Hollis's face was appealing, and I figured I could use the practice. Working out with Khai in Aeden had been interesting, but no one was tougher than my parents. If I wanted to be in top form, and I did, then I needed to be training with them.

It seemed like a good idea, right up until the moment I found myself flat on my back, my mother's bare foot at my neck, my eyes staring up into the business end of a bokken. Normally, this would have been the point where I would have conceded defeat. But this wasn't a normal day, and I wasn't the same awkward girl who had trained with my mother four months ago.

I closed my eyes, going deep, and found the center of my aura. Then, I exhaled forcefully, expanding the energy field around me quickly and violently. Her wooden practice sword clattered to the floor as my mother was lifted off of me and thrown backwards several feet. Before she could recover, I kipped up onto my feet and spun into a graceful Lasair counterattack. Quickly, I whirled around her, tapping her lightly on one cheek in a mock punch as I vaulted over her chest and aimed a kick at her knee. If this was a real fight, she would have been disabled and disoriented, unable to recover for at least thirty seconds.

As it was, she simply threw her hands out to the side and groaned.

"I surrender! I can see you've learned some new moves since the last time we fought."

"Yes, but you're not supposed to use your powers in training," my father admonished. His split attention earned him a bloody lip as Gawen's fist managed to catch him by surprise. My father growled and went after Gawen like a steam train. Gawen's eyes widened, but he didn't back down.

He gave a good fight, but still wound up on the floor a few moves later.

"If not here, then where? How am I supposed to know my limits, if I can't practice in a safe space?" I cajoled, helping my mother up.

"No magic, not in here. Another person's dojo is no place to test your powers," my father scolded.

"Then can we go outside?" I asked hopefully.

"Ana," Mom warned. "Give it a rest. The whole point of this is to see if you can best me without your powers."

"Yeah," Hollis called out nastily, mocking me from across the room where he was lifting weights. "Maybe if you'd had the right skills, you could have helped Khai."

"You take that back," I yelled, striding towards him.

"Just ignore him," Jules said, placing a calm hand on my shoulder. "He's just pissed because he's scared."

I eyed Hollis, who'd gone back to pretending to ignore us. "You think? Hollis, scared?" His aura did look jumpy. Something was definitely bothering him, even more than the day before. What had changed?

"Look," my father said, dabbing a cloth against his lip. "If you all think you're coming with Siri and me on this next phase of the mission, then you'd better get a few things straight." Jules and I straightened to attention, and Hollis sat up on the bench. "There will be no in-fighting. Whatever dramas you have going on between you, they end now. Today. The only thing that matters is the mission, you got that?"

"That means you will listen to Alec and me, and do whatever we tell you do," Mom said, backing him up. "If I tell you to sit down, you sit. It Alec tells you to run, you run. We can't save Khai and the others if we're busy worrying about you. We need to know that you can all behave like grownups. As warriors. Can you do that? For Khai?"

Chastised, we mumbled our assent.

"What's that? Can't hear you," Dad said, holding a hand to his ear.

"Yes," we all said more loudly.

"Good." Mom nodded, looking pleased. "Then I think next we should work on- Oh, hold a minute." She tapped her chat and looked off into the distance. "Yes? He did? Are you sure? Okay. We'll be right there."

She ended the call and turned to my dad. "Callie's gotten one of the men to tell her everything." She smirked. "Apparently, he sang like a bird when she-" She broke off, remembering she had an audience. "Never mind. I'll tell you on the way there. Everybody else, stop gawking and get back to practicing. I want you to all put in another hour of sparring, then hit the caf for some fresh fruit and protein."

She laid a hand on my father's shoulder. "Come on, Alec, you're not gonna believe what I have to tell you."

Hollis was already back at the weights, the repetitive clanging getting on my nerves. I watched my parents leave, wanting to hear what was going on. But they'd just given us strict orders, and we'd all agreed to follow them. Maybe eventually I would need to break that promise, but now wasn't that time.

I turned to Gawen and Jules.

"How about we practice fighting two on one? Jules, I've shown you some basic defensive moves, but things change when you're being ganged up on – and the warpers aren't always going to fight fair."

"I'm in," Jules said, grinning. "Gawen?"

"Sure, just tell me what to do," he said, barely paying attention.

"Okay, well, why don't you two come at me? I'll show you a few basic moves."

In a group fight, Lasair was really the best technique. However, the fae martial art was too complex to pick up in a couple hours, even for athletes like Jules or Gawen. Similar to capoeira, it could take years for someone to really master it. I should have known – my family were all expert Lasrach warriors, while I often still fumbled the more advanced maneuvers.

Instead, I focused on keeping it simple. The first time they came at me, I used Judo, showing them how the forms were designed to send down opponents swiftly, giving you time to run away while they lay stunned on the mat. The second, Krav Maga involved a bit more brute force. Focusing on quick, painful jabs to vulnerable parts of the body, Krav Maga left people in too much pain to come after you. You needed to make sure you delivered the blows with full force – otherwise, you'd have made some very angry, very vengeful, enemies. After running through several variations of both techniques, Jules and I laid into Gawen, giving him a chance to put learning into action. Hollis came over and leaned against the wall, scowling as he watched.

"You want to lend a hand?" I asked breathlessly. "Give them some pointers."

"Not really," he said, crossing his arms over his chest.

Jules cracked her neck and bounced up and down on the balls of her feet. "Okay, my turn. I think I've got the hang of this. Come at me."

Gawen and I circled her, probing for vulnerabilities. I tested her, striking out with one leg which she easily deflected. "Good," I said. I ran at her, aiming open-handed punches at her face, ribs and kidneys. Each time, she managed to block me. I spun and rolled, coming up on her other side, but she'd anticipated my move and grabbed my wrist even as it grazed her cheek, pulling me towards her to flip me over her shoulder. I lay on the floor, grinning like an idiot for a moment. Then, I rolled onto my stomach to watch her fighting Gawen.

Gawen's moves were unpracticed, rough, but what he lacked in fluidity he more than made up for his size and power. His long limbs gave him an advantage over Jules that I could never have, and she found herself quickly losing ground. She was about to lose, and she didn't even know it. I almost shouted out a warning as his arm came around her shoulders from behind, but stopped myself. She needed to learn, and with fighting the best way to do that was by experience. Muscle memory, my mom called it. Feeling a movement, the body would react faster and better the next time. And the time after that.

This time, though, Jules was too slow. Gawen's arm came around her as if he was going to choke off her air, and then he grabbed her arm and hooked a leg around her knee, sending her to the ground and pinning her in a painful position of loss in one easy motion. Impressed, I decided I would have to take back what I'd been thinking about his awkwardness a moment before.

I pushed myself up, ready to congratulate them both and go over what they'd done wrong, but I didn't get the chance. Before I could even speak, Hollis took Gawen down in a powerhouse Glima move, a staple Viking style of grappling we'd both learned as children. I was very, very familiar with that move. I couldn't count the number of times Hollis had taken me down with it.

I hated it.

"What the hell, Hollis?" I yelled, frustrated.

"Yeah, really," Gawen said, rubbing his head. We'd been practicing gently, taking care not hurt each other, but it appeared Hollis hadn't been holding back. He knew better, and I said so.

"Whatever," he ground out. He stabbed a finger in the air towards Gawen. "You. Keep your hands off Jules."

"Excuse me?" Jules exclaimed from behind him, planting her hands on her hips.

He rounded on her, furious. "You heard me. You're done here. Go home, Jules. Go back to school. You're not trained for this."

"You can't tell me what to do."

"Like hell, I can't. You think you're ready to fight warpers? Just because you had some training from my sister?"

"Yeah. I do. We're not family, Hollis. You can't tell me what to do."

"Look at yourself, Jules. You just got owned, by a college student with no training."

"Hey!" Gawen exclaimed, but Hollis kept talking, relentlessly hurling words at Jules.

"Every time you and Ana go off together, somebody gets hurt. She's always been the weakest link in our family, and you're just a human. You're not strong enough to handle what's coming."

I heard it almost before my eyes processed what I was seeing. Jules' palm smacked into Hollis' cheek and his head rocked back.

Finally speechless, he held his cheek in shock.

"You slapped me," he said dumbly.

"Don't you ever call Ana weak again. She is ten times stronger, and better, than you'll ever be. Just human?" she asked, and then repeated herself, bellowing the words a second time. "Just human?! How dare you. You racist, sexist, ableist freak."

Hollis didn't say a word, just stood there looking dumbfounded. Eyes wide, he continued rubbing his cheek. Jules stared back at him, eyes narrowing.

I'd seen that look before. It wasn't good.

She stomped her foot and shook both her fists in fury. "Well? Don't you have something to say?" She waited barely a moment, and then plowed on, demanding. "Apologize!"

"Jules, I-"

"Not to me, to your sister, you idiot!"

He dropped his hand and turned to me, shoulders slumped.

"Ana, I didn't mean to say-"

"Oh, Hollis, your cheek!" I exclaimed, interrupting him. Green and black veins radiated throughout his jowl where

Jules' palm had made contact, and exquisitely delicate sprigs of tiny green leaves had erupted from the skin, as if his earth power were bursting from within in defense of Jules' anger. "Let me see."

I placed my own hands around the area, gently probing what I felt there. And it wasn't Hollis' power. It felt out of place. Foreign. Someone else's energy.

"Jules," I murmured.

"What?" she said, thinking I was calling her over. Without words, I showed her his cheek.

"Geez, Hollis, those are some crazy defenses you've got there. Glad I'm not an earth fae."

"Jules," Gawen began. He was seeing something of what I was sensing, I could tell from the pitch of his voice. But I wasn't sure this was the time to talk about it. Not in front of Hollis, not when things were still so raw between them. So I hushed him, shaking my head and widening my eyes, and sent some healing energy into Hollis. Almost instantly, the leaves began to shrivel, the veins in his cheeks receding and fading.

"Can someone explain to me what's going on?" Hollis asked, still sounding dazed.

"I think Jules rattled you good, that's what I think. Why don't you go get yourself a smoothie, like Mom said? We'll catch up with you in a minute."

"Okay, I guess. Five minutes, okay? Mom didn't want any of us to overdo it." Hollis' natural leadership couldn't help asserting itself, even when he was in a fae-fueled plant coma.

"Yes, Hollis. Five minutes. We'll catch up. Go get some juice. Green, if you can find it. Trust me, you need it."

Chapter 12

Hollis was no sooner out the door than I turned on Jules.

"Do you have any idea what you've done?"

"I'm sorry, I know I shouldn't have slapped him but- What?" Jules stared at me, confused, as I waved her words aside with some pretty impressive jazz hands.

"Jules, you can slap Hollis any day, as far as I'm concerned. No, I mean, do you know that you just used earth powers?"

"What?" She said, stumbling as she backed up. "I- No! That was Hollis."

"No, Jules," Gawen said, standing behind her and placing his hands on her shoulders. "That was you."

"But I'm not fae. I don't have any powers. Ana, tell him. You've known me my whole life. My only superpower is the ability to run a mile in under five minutes."

"I told you before, I was sensing earth energy in you, remember?"

"Yeah, but I thought you meant..." She sagged against Gawen and he propped her up. "I thought you meant I was getting in touch with my hippie side. You know, after all that hiking? I never thought you meant I'd have actual *powers*."

She said the last word with hushed reverence, her eyes widening.

"I didn't want to freak you out before, especially since I wasn't sure. But Jules – those leaves on Hollis' cheek, they weren't his. The energy was different. You did that."

"But how?"

"I don't know."

"I think I do," offered Gawen, who'd been silent all this time. "Fae abilities can be accessed consciously, but they are also triggered by emotion. Maybe you always would have eventually accessed earth powers, Jules. Or maybe, your body adapted to match the object of what you wanted most."

I shook my head, trying to head Gawen off, but it was too late.

"Hollis? You think I want to be like Hollis?" She spun to face him.

"Well, not like him, exactly," he said, palms up in a gesture of submission.

"Not helping, Gawen," I warned.

Jules' eyes narrowed. "You think I still want him, don't you?" She whirled back towards me. "You, too, right?"

"Well, you know, you-"

"I am *not* chasing Hollis Ward!" she screeched, stamping her foot. Begonias sprung up from the hardwood floor around her sneaker, but she didn't notice. "I won't!"

"But you do have feelings for him," Gawen said softly.

"Look what you've done to the floor," I said gently, pointing down.

Jules rolled her eyes and huffed, then looked down. Her jaw dropped, and her eyes welled up. "No," she whispered. "I don't want to anymore. I can't." She looked up at me, tears running down her cheeks. "He doesn't love me, Ana. And now I'm an earth fae, like him?"

"There've been other humans, getting powers, you know? I think we're all a lot more alike than anyone ever knew," I offered lamely.

"Fine, whatever, sure. But to be like Hollis, that way? How am I ever supposed to get over him, Ana? What am I going to do?" Jules sunk to the floor, wrapping her arms around her knees, and I rushed to her side.

"Maybe you're not supposed to," Gawen said, looking down at us.

"Huh?" We gawked back up at him.

"Maybe, you're not supposed to," he repeated. "He's not indifferent. Not even remotely. I know what a guy looks like when he wants someone he can't have. And his energy? It's all kind of wound up."

"Are you sure?" I asked. "You don't think he's just freaking out about Khai?"

Gawen shook his head. "Nah. His whole aura shifts when Jules is around. It's her. You guys are made for each other. He just doesn't know it."

Jules laughed bitterly. "Care to tell him that?"

"I don't think he's interested in hearing anything I have to say. He's barely tolerating my presence here. Maybe just give him some time? Focus on getting Khai back and-"

"Screw that," I interrupted. "What if we never get Khai back?"

"Ana!" Jules protested, grabbing my hand. "You can't mean that."

"No, seriously. I mean it. What if we don't? And what if we all get caught, or worse, die tomorrow? Wouldn't you regret having waited? I don't want to live like that anymore. You know, behaving, waiting for permission. From now on, if I feel something, want something, I'm going for it. Because life is fragile. No one on this planet is immortal. Nothing is permanent or guaranteed."

"Okay," Jules said, leaning back and cocking her head as she looked at me. A smile burst forth, like the sun from behind a line of storm clouds. "You've changed."

"I know." I beamed back at her. "We both have. It's good, right?"

Her lips quivered, but the smile stayed in place. "I guess it is. Having powers – am I becoming fae?"

"I don't know." I looked at Gawen for his opinion.

"Science is still trying to figure it out. No humans seem to have gone full-on fae yet, but the line between the species is becoming fainter every day. We've always had very similar DNA chains. I mean, we can procreate together – we're not so different, like Ana said."

Jules pretended to gag. "Procreate?"

Gawen blushed. "Shut up. You know what I'm saying."

"Yeah, Gawen, I do," she said, eyes twinkling. "Okay, so what now?"

"Well, why don't we practice? See what you can do?" I asked.

"In here?"

"Probably not a good idea. Although we could start with those plants there. I don't think the starseeds will appreciate our gardening efforts in their training area."

"Right. Um, what do I do?" she asked.

"Well, you've heard Mom's story about when she and Dad first met, right? How he bound her with vines and made her get rid of them herself to test her?"

"Oh yeah, I love that story!" Jules laughed.

"Me, too," I grinned. "Well, she says she talked politely to the plants and asked them to withdraw, but the key was that she pushed her light out into them, first." I looked at her expectantly.

"You want me to use light?" Jules sounded confused.

"Yeah, your light. Kind of like your aura," Gawen supplied.

"Right," I said. "Imagine you are filled with light, like the sun. It can be whatever color you want, just see yourself full of it. Then try pushing it out, towards the plant, see if you can connect."

She closed her eyes and concentrated, but nothing happened.

"I can't."

"Try again," I urged and waited, watching her breath slowly in and out. After a minute she shook her head.

"Nothing's happening."

"So far her displays have required contact," Gawen mused. "Maybe if you touch them?"

Jules grunted but did as he'd suggested, kneeling next to the begonias and stroking them gently with her hand.

"Please? I don't want to ruin the starseeds nice floor. Please, can't you just, I don't know, go away? Pretty please?" She looked up at me, shaking her head again. "I don't know what to do Ana, it's still not-"

"Shh!" Gawen whispered, pointing at her hand. The flowers were merging into her skin, veins of green, pink and coral trailing up her arm, feeding into her blood. In moments the plants had disappeared, the floor shining and whole, as if it had never been permeated by living matter.

"Holy cow," Jules muttered. "Did I just absorb a flower?"

"You did," I said, equally awestruck. I'd never seen anyone's earth magic work quite like that. I didn't know if it was something new, or simply that I hadn't known many earth fae outside my own family – regardless, it had been pretty amazing. "How do you feel?"

Jules flexed her hand. "I feel...awesome, actually. Like I could run twelve miles."

"Let's not be hasty," Gawen joked.

"No. I'm not in the mood for a run, either. But that gives me an idea. Come on, guys." I got up and led my friends downstairs and outside, back to the walking trail along the Charles. Soon, we found ourselves among bushes, grasses and trees, amidst the riverside park.

"Behold, your own private training ground," I said with a majestic wave of my arm.

Jules chewed her lip. "What should I do?"

"Whatever you want. Make something grow bigger? See if you can move some earth? Play around."

"Okay. I guess I can do that. Practice makes perfect, right? How should I start?"

"Well, we know emotion makes you trigger your power. But it's more helpful to be able to do what you want, when you want. Remember how you helped me practice on the Long Trail all those hours?"

"Boy, do I ever."

"Well, now it's your turn. What do you want to start with?"

"I guess something defensive would be cool. I'd love to be able to do to Hollis what your dad did to your mom all those years ago."

"You and me both! Alright, Gawen, you want to be her target?"

"Why not you?" he mock-whined.

"Because I'm going to give her pointers." I winked.

"Plus, you're a guy," Jules deadpanned.

"Yeah, what she said," I laughed.

Gawen laid down in the dirt and closed his eyes. Amazingly, he dropped off into a deep, snoring slumber within moments.

"Is there anywhere he can't sleep?" Jules wondered.

"In the water? He must have made the water polo team somehow," I said.

"Right." She inhaled slowly. "Well, here goes nothing."

She placed her hands on the dirt next to his arm and closed her eyes.

"So, um, I just call the plants to me?"

"I think so. Ask nicely, I guess?"

"Okay," she said in a singsong voice.

"Try thinking about how much you love gardening – you know, those great tomatoes you and your dad grow every summer. Try that. Remember how nice it feels to have your hands in the dirt, to see the little seedling start to burst from the soil, to-"

"I got it," she murmured. And she did have it. Bright, spring green tendrils were bursting forth from the earth, caressing her hands before they sped towards Gawen. Within moments, he was encased in a living shroud of green. Tiny yellow flowers began to open as the vines continued to twine around him, his face beginning to disappear from view.

"Um, Jules?"

"What?"

I pointed at the tendril creeping over Gawen's nose.

"Oh!" She lifted her hands from the ground, and the vines stopped their procession of growth. "Now what do I do?"

"Same as in the dojo. Ask the plants nicely. See if you can get them to return to the earth this time."

I watched her concentrate, whispering softly to the plants as they obeyed her command and sank back into the earth. Well, most of them. Some vines couldn't seem to resist connecting with Jules, feeding her their energy. Her body drank them in, and I watched her aura grow brighter. Radiant with light.

Like a fae.

For a moment, I couldn't speak, struck dumb by the magnitude of what I was seeing. Jules *was* becoming fae. Or maybe something new, something more than fae? It was amazing. It was beautiful. And it was all happening to my very best friend.

Overcome, I wrapped her in a hug.

"What's this for?" she asked, chuckling even as she hugged me back.

"I'm just so glad we're friends, that's all. And I'm so happy for you."

"Why, because I'm becoming like you?" she asked, snark creeping into her voice.

"No, because you're becoming like *you*," I said, my voice thick with emotion. "You're so freaking bright Jules, I wish you could see it. Your light, it's amazing."

Gawen snorted, a porcine snuffle of a sound, and rolled over onto his side, still fast asleep. Jules and I giggled and moved further away, not wanting to wake sleeping beauty. She practiced raising vines several more times, each time with more speed and proliferation than the previous attempt.

"I think you've got the hang of it, you can practice more later. Think you're ready to play with some dirt?"

"Like, dig a hole with my mind or something?"

"That could be useful – you could trip enemies with that. But I was actually thinking of more of a barrier – something you could hide behind if you needed to."

"Seems a bit cowardly, don't you think?" Jules said, cracking her neck.

"Not if people are shooting lightning bolts at you, or real bullets. I'm thinking it seems pretty useful. Remember, the best offense is a good defense."

"Ah. I see your point. Okay. So, um, how do I do that?"

"Good question. I'm no earth fae, remember? I've seen my grandfather do it – but he's got an affinity for stones. Still, you never know until you try, right?"

"Okay. I guess...maybe if I imagine playing with sand, like at the beach." She closed her eyes and took a few deep breaths, moving her hands in front of her like she was making a sand castle. Faster and larger than I ever would have imagined, a wall of clay snaked towards us from the river, crossing the path and rising towards us like a tidal wave.

"Holy-"

Jules opened her eyes and gasped. "I did that?"

"Mmhmm," I affirmed. We exchanged victorious smiles and high-fived each other, possibly squealing a little as we did.

"What the hell?!" An angry voice came from the other side of the wall. I couldn't see the person who'd spoken, the earthen barrier blocked my view, but I knew that voice.

Then, the clay was shattering, hard, moist pellets pelting me in the face as Hollis blasted the barrier out of his way.

"What in Odin's name is going on here?" he demanded, standing tall in the middle of the jogging path, arms akimbo.

"We're practicing," I said simply, daintily lifting one shoulder. "Use your eyes. And lower your voice, you're going to wake Gawen."

"Too late," the pale fae said, sitting up and rubbing his eyes. "Wow, Jules, what was that, a sea wall?"

She grinned at him. "Yeah, I guess it was."

"Sea wall?" Hollis repeated. "I don't understand. What are you guys doing playing with mud? Shouldn't you be training?"

"Duh. What do you think we were doing?" I said, enjoying myself more than was probably fair.

"What do I think?" Hollis shook his head. "You're not making any sense."

I puffed out my cheeks, exhaling theatrically. "Let me explain it then. Jules. Has. Powers."

"What?" He looked more confused than ever. Poor Hollis.

"Jules is an earth fae." I spoke slowly, like I was explaining things to a toddler. Emotions-wise, I figured that was about his age. "So we're practicing."

"That's impossible," he said, taking a step back. He eyed the cracked clay strewn across the ground like they were vipers that might strike at any moment.

"Not so," I said. "Totally possible. Totally happening. I got a whiff of it when in Montreal, but I wasn't sure what it meant. Now though... Those leaves on your cheek earlier – they weren't your doing. It was Jules."

"No way," he protested weakly.

"Way," Jules said, laughing.

Chapter 13

"But how can that be? Jules, you're just a regular human."

Jules eyed him like he was a moldy piece of food. "Don't make me school you again in how to respect me."

Hollis reddened. "I didn't mean that." He ran a hand through his hair, rubbing his neck. The gesture was straight out of our dad's handbook, something he always did when he was nervous or thinking. "You keep putting words in my mouth."

"No, Hollis, I'm pretty sure you're doing that all on your own," I said.

"No, I mean, you're twisting my words. You know I respect you Jules, I-"

"Ha!" She barked sarcastically. "You've got a lot to learn, Hollis, about how to treat a woman."

"I just can't win, can I? What do you want from me, Jules?" He said angrily.

"You know what I want," she whispered. Then she shook herself, drawing up straight. "Just treat me like any person, okay? Not your little sister's annoying friend, not some bimbo you dated. Just, another person, like we just met. Try treating me with a little dignity. Maybe get a little less comfortable assuming you know anything about who, or what, I am."

"Like I'm comfortable now?" he retorted.

"Perfect. Then you're on the right track," I said brightly and slapped him on the back. "Now, why don't you make yourself useful and teach Jules something about working with the earth element? So far, she's mastered growing vines and moving dirt to form a barrier."

"That wall was really her?"

"Yep, first try, too," she said proudly.

Hollis' eyebrows sprang up. "First try?"

"Mmm-hmm," I affirmed. "I'm telling you, she's amazing. Learning faster than I ever did. So, what can you teach her?"

Hollis' mouth worked, no sound coming out at first. He cleared his throat and tried again. "Plant growth. You can do it on command?"

"Yes. I don't even have to be angry anymore to do it."

"Can you do it at a distance?"

"At a distance? No."

"Okay, well, let's start with that. You can't always be close to an aggressor. You need to know how to throw your power."

"Sounds sporty. I like it," she said, doing a little dance and grinning coyly.

Hollis, all business now, made a long-suffering face and proceeded to launch into the particulars of calling up plants from a distance. He treated Jules with patience and deference, never touching her and answering every one of her questions. I knew he worked as a Teaching Assistant at McGill, and for the first time I was able to see him like that – not my know-it-all brother. Someone who could make a great teacher or leader someday, someone even I might actually want to listen to or follow.

"What's making you so happy?" Gawen whispered in my ear.

"Hollis," I whispered back. "Look at him. He's actually a really good teacher. I had no idea."

"Yeah. He's even managing to put his feelings for Jules aside. Pretty impressive."

"Feelings for Jules? What are you talking about?"

"Look at him. Check out his aura."

I watched my brother as he showed Jules how to call up vines from the trees, triggering them like a trap when he threw a rock below them. Before it could hit the ground, the rock had been snatched up and wrapped in a green cocoon ten feet above the ground.

Jules oohed and aahed, but that wasn't what made my jaw drop open.

How had I missed it?

True, I'd pretty much had no interest in looking at Hollis, like, ever. I'd had even less interest in his aura. Looking at it at first, I could see why. It was a dull, dependable blue and red. Strong and effective. Leadership hues. Rock solid, like his abs. Blech.

Like his emotions, he kept his energy wrapped tightly around him, simmering hot and cold just inches from his body. Bright, but contained.

So it was easy to see how I'd missed it.

The faint rays of pink that burst from his chest, every time he looked at her. Even when he tried to pretend he barely saw her. The way his hand opened, shining with pure golden light, reaching out towards her, and then clenched shut before she could notice the gesture.

"Holy crap. He likes her."

"Likes her? With that gold light? That's the surge, doll. Your brother is head over heels for that girl."

"Oh sure, now that she's turning fae he's all gaga for her. Good luck to him," I frowned.

"No, not just now. I noticed it back at HQ."

"Do you think he even knows?" I asked him. Gawen had a lot more experience reading people than I did.

"Of course he knows. He doesn't like it. But trust me, Hollis knows."

"What do I know?" Gawen and I jumped apart, trying to plaster innocent expressions on our faces while Hollis glared at us in consternation.

"How to, to, um, teach Jules the earthquake technique," I stuttered. Hollis' grey eyes narrowed, piercing me with his icy stare, but I dug in. "You know, like Mom? I know you don't do it much, but I'm sure you can show her the basics."

"Yeah, okay." He ran a hand through his inky black hair again, making himself look like he'd been electrocuted. *Gods, I miss Khai.* The thought ran through me like fire, stealing my oxygen. Thank Odin, Hollis and Gawen were both watching Jules at the moment. Again and again, she commanded the vines to lash out at each other and create various designs between the trees. Then, she tossed another rock at them, jumping up and down and clapping her hands delightedly when they snatched it mid-air.

"We've created a monster," Hollis said quietly, sounding pleased.

"Not you. Not me. Anansanna. Humans all over the planet are changing, you've heard the news," I reminded him.

"Yeah. I guess I just never really believed it," Hollis said. "I mean, I never met one before. Did you?"

I shook my head, but Gawen smiled. "Actually, yeah. Quite a few. There are more than you'd think. You just have to know where to look."

"Or how to look," I said, winking at him.

He laughed. "That, too."

"Jules," Hollis called. "That's enough. Put the vines away." He strode over to where Jules was standing and watched her force the wild plants to retreat back into the ground.

"We should probably go," I said, watching Hollis start explaining to Jules how to make the ground shake. "I hate earthquakes."

"Good call. And a natural water fae reaction," Gawen agreed, shuddering theatrically.

"Hey, guys!" I called out, "We're gonna head back. See you later."

They waved, barely noticing our departure. I looked up at Gawen as I linked arms with him, strolling south along the river's edge. "How so? The reaction, I mean."

"Oh, you know – water, earthquakes, tsunamis. Too much earth energy can throw a water fae really off balance, though the right amount can help keep us steady and grounded."

"Interesting. No wonder my family drives me nuts."

"Yeah, you do have kind of an overabundance of earth magic in your home. It's probably why you didn't come into your powers for so long. Too much grounding, your energy couldn't flow freely."

"Oh, I never thought of that." We walked on in silence for several minutes, each of us lost in our own cocoon of thoughts.

Watching two swans drifting on the Charles, one trailing lazily after the other, I couldn't help remembering what Gawen had said about Hollis and the surge.

"Hey, Gawen?"

"Mmm?"

"How can you be so sure Hollis knows what he's feeling? I mean, that he doesn't like it?"

"Well, he's not acting on it, is he? I mean, he ended it with Jules pretty badly, didn't he?"

"Well, yeah, but... Is it possible that he's so cut off from his emotions that he doesn't even know what he's feeling?"

"I doubt it. He's not cut off, he's just..."

"Contained. I know, I saw it." I sighed. "Then why do you think he's been so awful to Jules?"

"My guess? He's mad at himself for wanting what he can't have."

"What do you mean? No one's stopping him from being with Jules except himself."

"Come on, Ana. Jules is your best friend. What would you do if he hurt her?"

"Hate him." I chewed my lip. "Kind of like I've been doing."

"Exactly, all they did was make out a few times and have a fight. Imagine if it got serious and ended badly."

"I never thought of it like that."

"Yeah, well, I'm sure Hollis has," he said bitterly. "Probably thousands of times. But Jules is like family. A guy knows better than to mess with that. I bet it's tearing him up inside, knowing what he wants and feeling like he's not allowed to cross that line."

I eyed Gawen suspiciously. "Sounds like you're speaking from experience."

"Maybe I am." He shrugged. "Or maybe I'm just a really great empath."

I barked with laughter, clarity dawning.

"Oh. My. Gods. You have feelings for Reenah."

"No." Gawen shook his head so vehemently that strands of pale hair came loose from the long braid trailing down his back. "I don't. We're family."

"Except you aren't. Not really. No more than Hollis and Jules are brother and sister."

He looked at me, incredulous. "I've bought Reenah tampons. More than once. Can Hollis say the same?"

"Definitely not. But so what? She has a body. You know it. She knows it. And you like it." I hip checked him and sang out, "Gawen likes Reenah!"

"Stop it, Ana." Waves began to churn along the shore of the river, but I paid them no mind.

"Not until you admit it. You like Reenah. Deeply. Madly. Passionately," I called out gleefully.

"I do not!" He denied it, but his skin was flushed red from his neck to the roots of his hair. He was embarrassed, and he was mad. "Take it back."

"No." I stroked my chin. "In fact, maybe I should call her, have a little chat." Water sloshed over my head, soaking me. "Hey!"

"It's not your secret to tell," Gawen said petulantly, smiling a little now.

"So you admit it is a secret, then?"

He nodded reluctantly. "But you can't tell her. Someday, maybe, I'll tell her. But now, with her parents back..."

"I get it. You want to give her space. Just don't give her too much, hey? Before she left, you were kind of a jerk."

"I know." He sighed. "Just, the thought of never living with her again kind of made me a little crazy. I'd adjusted to the fact that we couldn't have a relationship, but I thought as long as she was near...I could handle it, you know? Now, with her parents back, everything's changed."

"For the better, don't you think?"

"Yeah." He didn't sound convinced. "I'm happy for her. I am, really." He pasted a smile on his face and pointed to it. "See?"

"Oh, Gawen." I threw an arm around his waist, smiling up at him. "You're going to be fine, I promise. Everything's going to work out."

"How can you know that?"

I thought of Reenah's parents, aged and damaged. I thought of Khai, struggling in the hall below The Raven's Grimoire against his captors. Then an earlier memory of Khai, rolling down the stairs of my house, tangled with Hollis and tasing him unconscious. Laughing. Sparking. The way I needed to remember him. The way I wanted to see him again.

I would not think of him any other way.

105

I realized Gawen was still waiting for an answer and shrugged. The answer was simple. "Because it has to."

Chapter 14

Gawen and I were nursing a couple of fruit smoothies and nibbling on trail mix, watching an old Alien rerun on the Holo-vid screen in my suite for "research purposes" when my dad barged in. His hair was wild, his violet eyes shining brightly even though he wasn't in the dark. They locked onto me with purpose.

"Good, you're here. No one's answering their chats, had me worried. Where's your brother?"

"Um, probably in the caf. Or maybe still outside training with Jules."

"With Jules?" That last bit caught my dad off guard. Apparently even he had noticed the tension between them.

"Yeah." I sat up, putting my food down on the table and smiling brightly. "She's turning earth fae, can you believe it? She's got powers, Dad! Real powers!"

"Jules? Has powers?" He blinked, surprised. "That's- well, it's convenient, that's for sure. I'm not going to deny that I was worried about bringing her along, but if she's got powers, that puts my mind at ease a bit. Of course, I doubt Keith would see it that way." He trailed off, frowning at the thought of Jules' own father. Then, he ran a hand through his hair, shaking it like a dog after a bath. "Never mind. Look, I need you kids to get your gear together. We're moving out. I'll go find Hollis – tell your mother where I went when she gets back."

"Um, okay." Gawen and I looked at each other as my father spun out of the room.

"Dude, your dad is intense."

"Yeah. Sometimes. He can be fun, too, though. I swear!" I laughed, seeing the look of doubt on Gawen's face. "Really. But you know, once a Light Guard, always a Light Guard. He's better when my mom's around. She kind of brings out the best in him."

"I noticed. It's cool, if you ask me. They're a good match, the great Siri Alvarsson and her warrior."

"Shut up," I said, socking him in the arm. "They're just normal people."

"Oh sure, totally normal." Gawen rolled his eyes. "Normal people, who basically saved the world and changed it forever. Just a regular couple of kids who were the reason people like your friend Jules now are turning fae."

"Whatever. Go pack your stuff, drama queen," I smirked at him and pointed towards the door.

In three long strides, he reached the exit but paused, his hand on the doorknob.

"Where do you think we're going, anyway?"

I rubbed my hands over my face, bringing them into a prayer position against my chin as I considered. I had no idea. Besides, there was really only one answer.

"To war, Gawen. We're going to war."

"Now who's the drama queen?" He laughed, slipping out the door before I could throw a handful of nuts at him. I stuck my tongue out at the door as it shut behind him, then leaned back to stare at the ceiling.

Like Gawen, I wondered where we were headed. Unfortunately, the plain white paint above held no answers. Not for the first time, I wished I'd inherited some of my mom's ability to see the future. Our ancestor, Skuld Norna had held the power, and so had my mom. Her visions only really had to do with earth disasters, so it probably wouldn't have come in so useful, anyway. My brother, of course, had inherited some of the gift, too. While he couldn't have outright visions, he did seem to know things before they happened, like a sixth sense that made it almost impossible to surprise him. I smiled to myself, realizing that I'd been able to surprise him more times in the last couple of months than I had in the last ten years.

My water abilities certainly had come in handy. Now, if we could just find Khai, everything would be all right.

"Packed already?" Mom asked as she breezed into the room.

I startled and blushed. She'd caught me off-guard.

"No, I, um... I was spacing out," I admitted. "I'll throw everything together now. It's not like I have a lot of stuff."

She nodded, already heading into her own room. "Just make sure you don't leave anything behind," she called. "I don't believe we'll be coming back here."

Not coming back here? How far were we headed? Wouldn't we have to come back with anyone we rescued? Questions piled up in my brain like logs jamming a river. Wanting answers, I hastily tossed my things into my pack. I stripped off my sweaty shirt, pulled on a fresh one, and layered up with a soft long-sleeved fleece over clean leggings.

"Ready!" I yelled, heading back out to the sofa to pull on my sneakers. My mom threw her own bag onto the sofa from behind me, startling me again.

"Jumpy, huh?" she asked, hiding a grin.

"A bit," I conceded as she sat down next to me. "Excited, but nervous, too, you know?"

"I do," she said, taking a deep breath. "Listen, Ana, I meant what I said before. You will not do anything crazy on this mission, do you hear me?"

"I'm not a kid, Mom. You don't have to worry about me."

She closed her eyes. Shook her head, like I was being totally dense. "I will always worry about you, even when you're two hundred and forty-eight." She reached over and ruffled my hair. "You're my baby, you know?"

"I know," I mumbled.

"Good. Now come here." She opened her arms and I fell into them, just like I had when I was five. Like I would when I was two hundred and forty-eight. She was right. I would always be her baby. No matter what. But that didn't mean I wanted to feel like one. Hugging my mom was dangerous, because even as it released all sorts of happy familial love endorphins throughout my system, it made me feel soft. Too safe.

Exactly the opposite of the reality we were about to head into.

I extricated myself from her arms and tried to smooth my hair into a presentable array of curls. Like that would ever happen. Most of the time, I was pretty sure it looked like a bird nest that had been set on fire.

"So, where are we going, anyway?"

"Connecticut. Sharon."

"Who's Sharon?"

"Not who. Where. It's a small town in the Northwest corner of the state. Callie's arranged two large hovercraft to take us there, so if we leave now we should get there by three."

"Three? What time is it now?"

"Almost two."

"Oh, wow, I didn't realize we'd been training so long. So, it's not that far. Why wouldn't we come back here?"

"Callie's letting us take two hovercraft – the largest will return here with starseeds. The other will take us straight to the North portal. We're assuming anyone fae will need medical attention in Valhalla."

I swallowed. "You mean, like Khai."

She put her hand on mine. "I hope not. But we have to be prepared for anything. Callie is getting extra transports ready, too, in case we need more room. The smaller one only carries eighty people."

"Eighty? Jeez, Mom, how many people do you think we're going to find?"

"I don't know. But I don't want to have to leave anyone behind, either."

"Right. That would suck," I agreed, thinking only of Khai, his face as he'd told me to run, to leave him behind.

"Right!" she said, slapping my knee and making me jump. Again. She stood and started pacing. "Where are your father and brother, anyway? We should get going- Ah, speak of the devil."

The door to the suite had opened and Hollis had strode in, heading straight to his room without making eye contact with either of us. My father followed at a slower pace, looking amused.

"Everything okay?" My mom eyed Hollis' closed door with concern. You didn't need to be a water fae to see that something was bothering him.

Dad snorted. "I think the day of reckoning has finally arrived."

"Reckoning?" Mom looked confused, but then comprehension dawned. "He's met a girl? The girl?"

"Looks that way. And boy, is he pissed." Dad laughed.

"What happened?" I asked eagerly, propping my chin on the back of the couch. Dad looked at me, appearing to have just realized that I was in the room.

"Nothing."

"You're a terrible liar," I said.

"I am not. I run great undercover. Ask Bran," he said, referring to my grandfather, his former Commander.

"Can't lie to a water fae. Now, spill."

"Yeah, spill," my mom said, curling up on the couch next to me. My father opened his mouth to speak, but clamped it shut when Hollis came back into the room. "Later," he mouthed to my mom and I groaned, knowing I would have to wait, too.

Hollis' gaze roved over my father, mother and me; whatever he saw, he didn't like. His face shifted into a glower, shutting us out, and he stormed out without another word.

"Okay," drawled Mom. "I guess we can go now."

"You packed my stuff?" Dad asked, not sounding too pleased.

"Yep." My mom started to pull on a well-worn leather jacket, a tough looking item she'd claimed from Amber Slaight years ago.

"Rolled or folded?" Dad asked as he moved to help her.

"What do you think?" Mom laughed.

"Neither," Dad grumbled.

It was the same conversation almost every time they went on a dig. My mom was notoriously haphazard when it came to housekeeping, and her packing abilities weren't any better. My dad, meanwhile, well he wasn't OCD, just particular. He liked things a certain way. He blamed it on his military training, though Mom said it probably had more to do with his innate need to feel like he had control over his life. As a child, his whole life had been uprooted by the Dark fae when they killed his own mother and sister. The tragedy had forced him and his father to retreat to Aeden, leaving everything my dad knew behind. That day, he'd decided to become a Light Guard, to hunt down the Dark and protect other fae from having to go through what he had. It was also the day he'd lost the love of a mother – a heartache only the love of my own mother had been able to ease. Of course, he was much more light-hearted and relaxed now that the threat of the Dark was gone from our world. But now and then the old Alec Ward would surface – like when he worried about my safety, or when he was fighting, or packing a go bag.

"Ana, are you ready?" he asked me now.

"Yeah, of course. I was born ready." I could tell Dad disagreed, but he wasn't about to argue. No. Dad had shifted into Guard-mode, and that meant no teasing, no arguments.

We shouldered our bags and rode the elevator top-side. The lift doors slid open, revealing a windy rooftop where a sleek, brassy transport gleamed and hovered one story above the building with barely a sound. We were the only people on the roof.

"Where are the starseeds?" I asked.

"Already on board." My mother pointed to the sky. Another few hundred feet above us a second ship waited, the larger vessel shining like a drop of warm honey. "Both ships are equipped with full medical, but we are assuming we will find more starseed prisoners than fae. Our ship, the smaller ship, will take us back to the North Portal once we've completed the mission. Everyone else will come back here."

"Remember that," Dad said, both his words and his will pressing into mine "If we have to leave in a hurry, head for the smaller ship."

"Okay, yeah sure, of course."

"Good. Let's get on board, then," he said, sounding resigned.

"What about Gawen and Jules?" I said, not budging.

"We're here," Gawen said, stepping onto the roof with Jules.

"You're not having second thoughts, are you Ana?" my father asked hopefully, watching me closely.

"Oh no," I said, straightening my shoulders. "None."

My father wrinkled his nose, his mouth twitching to one side. "Well, it was worth a try. A father can hope, after all."

I patted his shoulder. "Come on, Dad. Let's go."

We walked up the gangplank, its rough rubbery surface gripping our shoes. I'd ridden on ships like this on school trips and visits to see family in Europe. The hoverships were pretty fast, and convenient for group travel since not everyone bothered owning a personal vehicle anymore. A lot of people figured it wasn't worth the bother, since you could borrow whatever you wanted from municipal lending garages. I knew that the government still had its own weapons and tactical vehicles like these, though, outfitted with weaponry and shields but it wasn't something that your average civilian ever saw. Tools of defense existed out of sight and mind, government backup plans that no one really ever considered would truly be necessary. War was an outdated concept and the world's armies had become mere shells of their former existence.

Clearly, though, the starseeds ran their own show and had their own means. I had to wonder what kind of gear these ships were outfitted with, what kind of weaponry or defenses. EMPs? Anti-flight dampeners? What kind of weaponry would they use against another starseed – enemies who could probably move ships with their minds?

My parents told us to find a seat and moved on to talk to the pilots. Jules found an empty group of seats on the port side, six cushy swivel chairs arranged around a circular central table. The tables almost gave the ship a cafeteria feel. I spotted Hollis in one corner going over a map with a couple of fae operatives. There was even a small self-serve refreshment stand in the corner. But the wholesome image was dispelled by the racks of weapons mounted along the opposite wall: stun guns; sonic blasters and localized EMP bombs were lined up like candy in a store. I spotted next-gen Kevlar vests, night vision lenses, hover boots, and countless other mercenary items that I couldn't identify.

Jules followed my gaze, then angled her chin at the groups of fae and starseeds seated nearby.

"I think everybody's been arming themselves," she said, pointing to the blank spaces were weapons and gear were missing. "What do you think? Should we..."

"I don't know." I caught my moms' eye as she came back out of the pilots' cabin and glanced at the weapons.

Looking resigned, she nodded and gave me a little wave.

"Okay, Mom says it's a go. Let's see what they've got."

We walked over and ambled along the wall, window shopping, trying to take it all in. I wasn't sure I'd ever seen so much firepower in one place, not even in Valhalla.

"I don't know what half of these are for. I've never fired a gun," Gawen said.

"Honestly? Neither have I," I said. "Little of my training has centered on modern weaponry. Swords, I can handle." I smiled as we arrived in front of the bladed weapons section. The only thing I would have liked more would have been a nice, solid bo staff. Not seeing anything like that here, I reached out and grabbed a small leather harness sheathing two short scimitars. I'd always had a fondness in my heart for the curved blades and often trained with them on Ayita's back, imagining myself as some sort of Arabian princess pirate, marauding through the desert. What can I say? I was an avid reader with a vivid imagination. Securing the leather straps over my shoulders, the blades crossed over my shoulder blades, the handles easy to reach on each side of my head.

"Flashy!" Jules exclaimed. "You look so badass. I've seen you handle weapons before, but most of them were made of wood."

"This is different, for sure," I agreed. "But then everything's been different since we graduated."

"You can say that again," she said.

"Here," I said, handing Jules a couple of grenades.

"I'm not sure I'm ready to go around blowing peoples' limbs off," she protested with a shudder, trying to hand them back. I pushed them into her hands.

"No. See the yellow circle around the bottom? These are flash bombs. Pull the ring to set a five-second timer, toss it, cover your ears and close your eyes. The light that goes off is so bright and loud no one will be able to see or hear a thing for several minutes. Just try not to blind the rest of us."

Then, I gave her a small army knife.

"Hide this in your bra. Gods forbid you're captured, chances are they won't pat you down to carefully there. You might be able to use it to get away – just don't try to fight back with it. Anyone who really knows how to use a knife will be able to take it from you in seconds and use it on you. And then I'll be regretting ever giving it to you. Here, Gawen, we should all have one."

"I'm not sticking it in my underwear," he warned.

I giggled. "Please, don't. Take two – one in your boot, one in your pocket."

"What's this do?" he asked, picking up a purple-ringed grenade.

"I don't know. Haven't seen purple before. Here, take this instead." I tossed him a metal wrist cuff, then handed another to Jules. "Auto-shield. Automatically raises a three-square shield wall when it detects incoming ballistics. Of course, it doesn't do much against a blade or most fae powers."

"How do I make it work?" Jules asked, giving her wrist a little shake.

"You don't. It's already armed, see?" I showed her the pale red shimmer along one edge. It's powered by your biofield. The minute it came in contact, it armed. Just try to keep that arm facing your enemies in a battle – it won't do much good if you're holding it on the wrong side."

"Cool," Gawen said, putting his bracelet on over his jacket.

"Not like that. It doesn't need to be exposed to work, but it does need skin contact."

"Right, stupid of me. Sorry." He pulled up his sleeve, putting the cuff around his wrist.

I grabbed another small pocketknife, shoving it down my shirt to nestle between my breasts. It might have been the first time I'd ever actually found them useful. Then, I spied a row of innocuous-looking black spheres, each about the size of a pomegranate, lined up like balls at a duckpin alley. I stooped to pick one up. They were heavier than they looked.

"What is it?" Jules asked. "Another bomb?"

"I don't think so." Turning it over, I spied the letters ANL, confirming my suspicion. "Just as I hoped. It's an ANL."

"A what now?" Gawen asked, laughing. I tossed it to him and he blanched. Still, he caught it easily.

"An aerial net launcher. Press down on that green tab and toss it above anyone you want to contain. The net deploys mid-air, titanium flex-wire traps anyone caught in its web – un-cuttable, inescapable."

"Nice," he said, hefting the ball in one hand. "Now that's my kind of weapon."

"I figured, since you like water polo."

"Honey, I don't just like water polo. I'm practically part fish."

"I know, saw your apartment, remember? Anyway, anyone who plays with balls as much as you do should be able to handle tossing an ANL. Grab that carrier there, it's designed to hold three safely."

"Awesome, will do." He loaded them up and pulled the carrier on like a messenger bag.

"Anything else?" Jules asked.

"Whatever you want, I guess. I like the look of this long underwear, myself." I gathered up the silvery silken material and looked around for a bathroom where I could pull on the bullet-proof stockings and shirt in privacy. Long ago, Dupont had gained a name for itself marketing bulky Kevlar vests to soldiers and law enforcement. Now, they specialized in undetectable, supremely comfortable and breathable body armor. Even with the world so safe, there was still a big market for the weightless armored long underwear among the sporting crowd, especially skiers and motorbikers.

"What's it do?" Gawen asked, picking up a pair and eyeing it doubtfully.

"Keep you from getting cut," I said drily. "Or shot."

Gawen raised his eyebrows and pocketed the underwear.

"You guys see a restroom anywhere?" I asked.

Jules pointed wordlessly over her shoulder to the snack corner as she thumbed through the leggings, looking for her size.

I left my friends to browsing the killing aisles and headed for the bathroom.

Chapter 15

The quarters were tight, but I had enough room to change easily, stripping down to my skivvies to pull on the silky armor and then redressing. *There*, I thought. *That should make Mom happy.* You wouldn't have known it to look at me, but ninety percent of my body was now protected from taking a bullet or knife.

I emerged from the bathroom, grabbing some veggie chips and fruit sodas for the table on the way back. Crossing the room, I made eye contact with Hollis. My parents had joined him and seemed to have decided on a plan of action. Everyone at the table was sitting back and joking around, enjoying the calm before the storm. I squinted at Hollis and gestured with my head for him to join us. If he had some knowledge about what we were heading into, he needed to share. He shook his head no, but I made another face and he rolled his eyes, relenting. Smiling in return, I continued on my way, plonking my bounty down on the table in front of my friends.

"Dig in. Don't know when we'll get our next meal. And try to behave."

Jules started to ask me what I meant, but clammed up when Hollis joined us.

"What?" he asked, turning a chair around so he could rest his arms over its back, giving me a surly stare.

"What's the plan?" I asked.

"You'll hear soon enough."

"Yeah, right. What Mom and Dad want me to know." I offered him a bag of chips and he tore into it, still not taking his eyes off me as he crunched down on a lavender sliver of kale. "If you really want to keep us safe, you'll give us some idea of what we're headed into."

Hollis stared into the bag of chips like he might find an answer among the turnips and rutabagas.

Finally, he puffed his cheeks out. "Why do I feel like I'm going to regret this?" he asked himself.

"You won't," I promised.

"Fine. I'll tell you what I know. But only so that you will relax and leave the real work to the professionals, okay? Mom and Dad want you guys to hang back, for everybody's safety. This is about Khai. Not you. Not me. Khai."

"Sure," I said, trying to smile as I lied through my teeth. "I get it. I solemnly swear to behave. Now tell us what you know."

"Okay, here, give me that napkin." He pulled a pen from his back pocket and started sketching. "This is where the warpers are conducting their experiments. The property used to be a pig farm, and the warpers allow the town to believe that they have converted the estate into an organic vegetable farm. In reality, of course, they've turned the pig sheds into prison facilities."

"These things are sheds?" I pointed at the massive rectangles he'd drawn out on the pale beige surface of the compostable hemp napkin, huge buildings that dwarfed the tiny square of the main house.

"Yeah, nice, huh? Pigs used to be farmed inside these buildings in cages, never seeing the light of day. No wonder people used to be so sick all the time, eating such low-quality food. Anyway, this is where we're going to come in. Our ship is landing here, and the starseed transport will be over here." He marked two x's in a field to the north, with the starseed transport seeming much closer to the sheds.

"Won't they see us coming?" Jules asked, leaning forward to get a better look at the picture.

"No. Satellite imagery shows that there's a stand of trees here and here. Plus, these ships are equipped with cloaking tech. If you're right next to the ship, you might notice a shimmer in the air, but otherwise we're virtually undetectable. That means, when you get off the ships, remember where you left them." He looked at me like I was inclined to get lost, but I refused to let him get to me.

"Okay, so we land. Then what?"

"Intel says there are three sheds. These two house starseeds. This one here," he circled the one closest to the main house in the south-west, furthest from the ships, "does double duty holding fae and the primary research labs."

"So that's where we're going," I said to myself.

"No. You three, you'll be hanging back with the medics to help escort the prisoners through the trees to the ships. That means you'll be waiting here, at the edge of the woods."

"But-"

"No buts, Ana. You promised Mom you'd listen."

I wrinkled my nose in distaste but said nothing, only nodded. Better for Hollis to believe I would cooperate. A few choice words from him and Mom might force me to stay behind on the ships -- something I couldn't allow to happen.

"So, what will you be doing," Jules asked, concern lacing the question, her big brown eyes looking up at Hollis. She still leaned over the table, her position exposing a vast expanse of creamy brown skin to his eyes. He swallowed and looked quickly down at the napkin, a flush creeping up his neck.

"I'll be with Mom and Dad, taking out the security in the main house before going to get Khai."

"So the rest of us wait for you before going in?"

"Going in?" Hollis repeated and I cursed inwardly at my mistake.

"I meant, in general, you know, before the other teams go in. Duh." I rolled my eyes for effect.

"Right." He eyed me suspiciously. "For your sake, I hope that's what you meant. Mom and Dad will skin you alive if they find out you're planning to disobey-"

"Yeah, I know, okay. I got it. Jeez."

"Good." Hollis puffed up a bit, looking back at his drawing. "Right. So. Everybody waits till they get the go-ahead from us via chat, then we have two teams storming each shed, one from each end. Your job is important, too, you guys. You'll be helping protect the medics in case anything goes wrong, and providing cover for the escapees. We're counting on you to get this right."

"You can count on us," Gawen said gruffly.

"I hope so." My brother pushed the napkin at me. "That's the plan. Stick to it, and everything should be fine."

He stood up, disentangling himself from the chair, and walked away.

"Gods, he's an arrogant stick in the mud." I sighed.

"He's not," Jules protested. "He's just careful."

"Especially when it comes to you two," Gawen agreed. "Me, I get the feeling he could care less about. But if anything happened to either of you... Well, not that I would ever wish anything like that on either of you, but it sure would be interesting to see."

"What would?"

"The imploding of Hollis Ward," Gawen mused.

I exploded with laughter. "Him? Hollis? Implode?"

"You know what they say about still waters," he said, popping a chip in his mouth.

"Yeah, but what do they say about mud?" I joked.

"Hey, watch it," Jules said lightly, taking a swig of her juice. "That could be my future mate you're talking about."

That set me off giggling, of course, and then she was laughing too, trying not to snort up her juice, and failing. My mom strode over, obviously thinking we'd lost our minds.

"Everything okay over here?" she asked.

"Right as rain," I quipped.

She crossed her arms over her chest. "I hope you're taking this seriously, Ana. We're heading into real danger here. You three, your job will be to help escort the people we rescue safely back to the ships with the medics. If we need to retreat quickly, you make sure you get on this ship. That's your most important job, as far as I'm concerned, you got that? You get back on this ship. All of you."

"Yes, ma'am," my friends mumbled. I nodded my head, which my mother took to mean I agreed. My great-grandmother had taught me that sometimes a nod could simply mean "I hear you." This was one of those times.

Of course, my mom knew that trick, too.

"Promise me, Ana."

"I promise! We will go with the medics and I will get back on the ship."

My mom relaxed and she gave me a hug. "Thank you. I don't know what I would do if I lost you."

She straightened up and looked at her watch. "Five minutes to arrival. Hope you're ready."

"I am. Look, I've got body armor and everything." I lifted my shirt to show her the silken layer underneath.

"Great. I better make sure everybody else is ready."

She stalked off and Gawen exhaled. "I still say your mom is seriously bad-ass. So, you've decided to "behave" after all?" He raised his hands, putting air quotes around the word.

"Not even one bit. I promised her we'd go out with the medics and we'd get back on this ship. I never said what we'd be doing in between."

My friends groaned.

"Shouldn't we listen to what they say? Your mom and dad, they have experience in this kind of stuff. Plus, you promised Hollis," Jules said, playing devil's advocate.

"I promised I'd behave. I never said *how* I'd behave."

"Good enough for me," Gawen said, cracking his knuckles.

"Me, too," Jules grinned.

"Hey, you don't have to come with me." Selfishly, I hoped they would, but I also worried about the danger I would be putting them in.

"As if," Jules protested. "Khai's my friend, too. I'm not standing back and letting you and Hollis have all the fun. Forget it."

"So what's the real plan?" Gawen whispered, leaning in.

"The real plan?" I drew out the napkin, considering our options. "We wait with the medics, here. When the other teams go in, we follow." I pointed to the back of the building Hollis had indicated as a fae testing ground. "Everyone else will be storming in, saving everyone, but we're going to be looking for just one person."

"Khai," Jules guessed, chewing her lip.

"Khai," I affirmed.

"But how do we find him?" she asked.

"Ana and I look for the dead zones," Gawen supplied. "The places that have no light, no fae energy. That's where they'll be keeping him. Ana and I will be able to sense it."

"Yeah, so long as our power doesn't get sapped first. Stay aware, and share anything you feel, even if it doesn't seem like a big deal."

"So that's it? We go in, look for Khai, hope for the best?"

"You have a better plan?" I asked.

"Nope." Jules held out her fist. "I'm in."

"Me, too," Gawen said, placing his fist against hers.

"You know it's not going to be that easy, right?" I asked, putting my hand out to match theirs.

"We've got this," Gawen said easily. "Go team!" he shouted, and Jules and I jumped, laughing.

"Go team!" the other teams cried, Gawen's spirit taking hold.

"Go team!" I yelled, joining in. "Bring 'em home!"

Chapter 16

"Coming in for landing," a woman's deep voice sounded over the speakers. "Ground teams, ready yourselves."

We picked up our packs and dutifully headed over to the team of medics. A young starseed loaded each of us with open duffels filled with what looked like rolls of parchment scrolls.

"Why do I feel like we're raiding the Library of Alexandria?" Jules muttered.

Joaquin, the young medic, laughed. "Haven't you ever seen an auto-stretcher before?"

"Only on my back," said Jules, probably remembering the time she'd suffered an in-game concussion last fall.

"Well, this is what they look like before activation. When you're ready to use one, just pull out a scroll, press the purple button here on the end and it will unroll and expand to hover at three feet above the ground. Once the patient is loaded, press the purple button again and the exo-gel will cover them completely, monitoring their vitals, supplying oxygen and keeping them from being jostled."

Jules shuddered. "That was the worst part. I couldn't get the taste of that gunk out of my mouth for weeks."

"Yeah? Well, it saves lives," the medic sniffed, sounding put out. I guessed he didn't like being told not everyone appreciated his kind of help. "Anyhow, once the person is en-gelled, you press the green button here, see?"

"What does that do?"

"Brings the stretcher back home, wherever we've set up the beacon. In this case, right here." He pointed to a blinking green light on a device at the far end of the hangar. Even as he spoke, one of the other medics was walking around the large room, pressing buttons in the center of each table. One by one, the tables and chairs receded into the floor, leaving a large empty space that would easily accommodate a thirty or more stretchers and attending medics.

"And these are for the fae we find? The other medics, their stretchers will go to their ship?" Gawen asked.

"Yep."

"Pretty cool," Gawen said, looking impressed. "What if we send someone to the wrong ship?"

The medic shrugged. "Tactical knows which teams are supposed to go where. Both ships return to HQ eventually, this one just heads north first. Either way, our people get home. Getting people out, that's what really matters."

"What about warper prisoners?" Jules asked. "Where do they go?"

"Same. But make sure they get a shot of this first, before you en-gel them." He pulled a small device out of a side pocket in the bag. "Knocks them out for a day. Plenty of time to get them back to HQ and secure them in comfortable quarters." Joaquin's eyes gleamed, like he was looking forward to bringing the warpers in.

"Did they take someone of yours, too?" I asked, feeling an empathetic tug.

Joaquin nodded. "Me, him, her. Pretty much everybody here has lost someone to the warpers. They've been poaching on starseeds for years now, building their reserves, planning something big. But since Callie lost the Star Mother a few years ago, it's gotten worse. They've gotten bold."

Almost imperceptibly, the ship came to a halt. The hangar doors slid open without a sound, the gangplank extending down to the ground. As it lowered, it shimmered, becoming practically invisible.

Squinting outside into the later afternoon sun, Joaquin squinted. "If something happens, if you can't find the ships, follow the stretchers. They'll lead you back!"

And then he was moving, loping down the walkway at an easy jog, disappearing among the tall rows of neglected corn. Dried out husks rattled, brown-leaved stalks rasping as fae and starseeds ran among them, but if you didn't know better you might have thought it was the wind. Quickly, we followed him, sticking close to the other medics as they made for the copse of trees at the south end of the field. I raised one arm and ducked my head, shielding my face from the razor-sharp leaves as I ran, thankful it was almost winter and I was wearing long sleeves. I followed the sound of feet pounding ahead of me, careful not to lag behind. Amid the stalks, it would have been easy to get lost or turned around. The tall grass-like plants closed in around me while sweat popped out in beads along my brow.

Just another minute. I chanced a glance towards the sky and was rewarded with a view of clear blue sky and tall naked treetops, along with a searing paper-like cut across my cheek.

"Ow!" I exclaimed, and instantly regretted it. So much for stealth. Mashing my lips together, I ran on, slowing as the corn gave way to forest floor, strewn with fallen leaves.

The rich, sweet smell of leaf-mold rose up to greet me, reminding me of petrichor after a summer rain. This was bounty, so much more so than the farmed aura of cultivation behind me.

I caught up with Jules and Gawen, both of whom had naturally outpaced me, and we walked as a group to rejoin the medics. There were more here than the ones from our ship. The larger transport must have arrived first, because there were forty or fifty medics here, crouched anxiously behind trees and boulders fifteen feet deep from the southern edge of the forest. Nestled among the shadowed wilds, we had a clear view of the compound while we remained obscured from view. At least, we hoped no one could see us.

I watched as my parents incapacitated several guards and led a tactical team into the farmhouse. I didn't see Hollis and assumed they'd sent him around the back of the house. I kept expecting to hear shots fired, but that wasn't the way the fae did business. Hand to hand combat was our forte, and always had been. We trusted our bodies, and our powers, to see us through any adversity. It was rare that they let us down. Bullets were the first defense of the powerless and the weak, my father liked to say. Only those without a clear line to Source, to the power of Anansanna, would feel entitled to take a life. The more filled with life and light you were, the less you wanted to rob another of the same. It was why so many fae lived as vegetarians, too. Still, I felt better knowing that my friends and I had armed ourselves. I didn't want to kill anyone, ever, but if it came down to a choice between a warper or my friends, I knew what I would do.

Any minute now, the other teams would be storming the sheds – impossibly long, sterile affairs sided in white wooden planks with aging aluminum roofs. No windows, just air exchangers mounted up high and a door at each end for coming and going. No emergency exits, because who cared about a few hundred pigs? Never mind that the sheds stored fae and starseeds, not livestock.

"We need to get into position," I whispered to Jules and Gawen. "Away from the others. Come on."

I tightened the strap on my bag of stretchers, making sure it sat on my hip, messenger style. I wasn't planning on leaving anyone behind. We slunk softly away from the medics, circling behind them to hide under a massive Eastern Pine. Eyes glued to the main house, I waited.

"Come on, come on," I muttered, feeling impatient.

"Steady," Gawen whispered, his hand on mine, pushing my palm into the rough bark of the tree where it rested. "It's not a race, Ana. We need to keep our heads."

I swallowed. He was right. I tried to think calm, centering thoughts.

I succeeded, too. Right up until the moment when several groups of people burst out from the farmhouse, streaming like water across the yard towards the sheds. As if on cue, more teams sprinted out of the woods, the bulk of them heading towards the two closest sheds. Heading towards the starseeds. Now was our chance. The research shed had two access points, but the fae teams were all coming from the house so they were only using one door. The rear door lay unclaimed, unwanted. Except by me.

"Time to move!" I hissed, heading straight it.

I was almost there when the door started to open, two young guys exiting, laughing. They had no idea what they were walking into. One of them opened a bottle, started to take a long drink, but his eyes widened when he noticed the teams of starseeds heading towards the other sheds.

"What the-"

He never got the last word out. The moment I'd seen the door open, I'd raised my hands. By the time it had shut behind them, I'd already sent out a pulse of pure, raw emotion. The shockwave of rage, fueled by my adrenaline and fear, knocked them off their feet. Arriving at their sides a moment later, I quickly scanned their energy.

"They'll live." Quickly, Jules pulled out a tiny metallic square, pressed it to one of their wrists and tapped it twice. Cuffs instantly emerged, wrapping tightly around the warpers wrists. She did the same to his friend.

"That should slow them down," I said, admiring her handiwork.

"Nice thinking. Wish I'd thought to grab some."

"Here, take some of mine. I have a ton." She tossed several of the tiny cubes at me.

"Thanks," I grinned, stowing them away. I looked at Gawen, who was trying to open the door.

"It's locked," he said.

"Here, try this." I ripped an ID badge from one of the men and flipped it to Gawen. He slid the card into the keypad and the lock clicked open.

"Down the rabbit hole we go," he murmured and pulled open the door. Inside, the hall was cement. Clean, but boring. There was no noise, no alarms, nothing to indicate the place was under attack.

We walked inside.

"You feel okay?" Jules asked.

"So far, so good. This part doesn't seem to be shielded from the Light," I said.

"Maybe none of it is," Gawen hoped.

"Maybe," I said.

Most of the doors here were open, leading to empty surgeries. It didn't look like a house of horrors. It looked like any other medical facility. Of course, we knew better.

"Where is everybody?" Jules asked.

I shrugged. "Dunno. Maybe they already cut out for the day?"

We came to a set of double doors. I peered through the glass window in the left door and grimaced.

"Not on vacation."

I moved aside, letting Jules and Gawen take a peek. What I'd seen was already seared into my brain. Men and women, barely dressed, unconscious and hooked to drips. Unlike the facility in Salem, I could tell this room wasn't a long-term kind of place. Surgeons and anesthesiologists milled around, talking with nurses, checking charts. A large surgical board covered one wall, naming procedures and operating room schedules. Apparently, we'd gotten here just in time to stop their afternoon lineup.

"They're prepping them for surgery," Jules hissed, disgusted, looking away.

"Not anymore," I vowed. My first examination had told me all I needed to know. There weren't any non-medical staff in that room and I wasn't about to wait for some to show up.

I burst through the doors, sending out pulses of energy and taking down several of the nearest doctors. The rest screamed, running for another set of doors on the other side of the room.

"Gawen, the nets!" I yelled, trying to knock out more of the doctors. They weren't fighting back, but we couldn't let them leave. Who knew what sort of alarms they might set off?

Too late, I realized that this room must have been shielded. I could feel my powers being sapped. I noticed one of the nurses scrambling for a red button on the wall and tried to throw her off her feet with a wave of power, but all I managed to achieve was a breeze of energy that rippled through her hair. Gawen had flung two of his ANLs above the rampaging herd, one after the other, and contained the bulk of the staff within the nets. Jules worked on restraining the others, vines bursting through the cement floors and racing around peoples' legs to first trip, then bind them. She'd entered the room last and seemed to still have a bit of juice left. Cursing the warpers' architects, I ran for the nurse, trying to beat her to the wall. She was too fast, too long-legged, and reached the wall before I could stop her, slapping one hand against the button. She grinned triumphantly at me just before my fist connected with her face, the smile never fading even as she slumped down to the floor.

Red strobe lights came on and a siren sounded, along with a calm recorded voice urging us to "Engage Lockdown Procedures." A pair of guards burst into the room. The first went straight for Gawen, no doubt assuming that the largest man in the room must also be the most dangerous. The second guard focused his eyes on me in anticipation.

"You," he snarled. A tremor of recognition when through me.

"Cougan," I said blandly, trying not to reveal my fear. The last time I'd seen him, he'd shot me and I'd lost Khai. This time, I had to do better.

He put his head down, coming at me like a battering ram as he pulled a large naval-style death knife from his belt. "You're going to pay for what you did to me."

I let out a string of curses under my breath, reaching behind my head and pulling the scimitars from their harness as I braced myself. "What's wrong, Gimpy?" I asked, noting his pronounced limp. "That broken leg didn't heal right?"

He lunged towards me, steel striking my blades. I had lifted them just in time, crossing them to block his attack. He was strong, limp or no limp, I knew that if I tried to match his strength I would lose. Instead, I bent backward, flipping and driving a foot into his stomach as I went. He stumbled back, but recovered quickly, coming at me again, striking out at my face. I got a close-up look at his blade, serrated edges and all.

I'd just barely managed to roll out of the way in time. I needed to get on the offensive, turn the tables, but he didn't give me a chance. Cougan was clearly just as skilled with blades and hand-to-hand combat as I was.

"It's just a matter of time, little girl," he said.

"Can't we just let bygones be bygones? I mean, you shot me last time." My voice came out shaky, like my breath, as I stopped another of his attacks. The clang of metal on metal rang in my ears. "It hurt really bad, I swear."

"You don't seem injured," he grunted, aiming a punch to my kidneys that I only just dodged.

"I heal fast," I said, shrugging as I spun around him and sliced through his shirt, a sliver of red blooming along his side.

He snarled, angrier than ever.

"You know who doesn't heal fast? Your boyfriend, what's his name?"

"David is healing just fine, thank you very much." I panted with exertion. The fight was wearing me out. I wasn't sure how much longer I could keep dodging his attacks. As big as he was, he moved like the wind.

"Not that loser. The other one. Khai."

At my friend's name, I lost my focus. How badly had Cougan hurt him? Had he taken his rage for me out on Khai?

That was all it took. A moment of distraction. Before I knew what had happened, Cougan had me pinned up against the wall with his body, his knife at my throat. In a second I would be dead, or maybe worse, his prisoner. I should have been using my training, trying to get away, but all I could think of was Khai suffering at the hands of this monster.

"What have you done to him?" I growled.

"Nothing I wouldn't do to you, sweetheart. Come on, I'll take you to him. I'm going to enjoy showing you just how friendly we've become."

I blanched. "I'll kill you first."

"Aw, so I can get under that pretty white skin of yours." He sneered into my face, his breath hot on my cheek, making it hard to breathe. I tried to stomp on his foot, but found only steel-toed boots. Instead, I jabbed a knee towards his groin, but couldn't find purchase, his body too close to mine. Too late, I realized he'd slowly been squeezing the air out of me with his other arm braced across my chest, slowly, imperceptibly suffocating me. White spots started to dance before me.

"Ana, your eyes!" Jules yelled. I looked up, trying to focus. Was she waving at me?

"I can't-" I was going to tell her I couldn't see, that I was losing focus. But then I realized what she had done. Not waving – throwing something at me.

Quickly, I scrunched my eyes shut and turned a cheek towards the wall, hoping to save at least one eardrum.

Light flared behind my lids and noise beyond comprehension shook every fiber of my being, only to be replaced by a high pitched whine of white noise. Cougan loosened his hold for only a moment, but that was all I needed. Quickly, I slammed my head into the bridge of his nose. As he stumbled backward, disoriented, I raised the scimitars over his head, slashing down. Killing him would be easy. At the last moment, I turned my wrists, slamming the butts of the handles into his crown, chest heaving as I watched him slump to the floor.

"I thought you were going to kill him," Jules shouted, her voice distant, coming through only on my right side and hard to hear over the lockdown warnings.

"I probably should have." I nudged him with one foot, rolling him onto his stomach. Before I could change my mind, I pulled his arms behind him, securing them with a pair of cuffs. "He's been torturing Khai."

"He told you that?"

I nodded. "Pretty much. Quick, let's get these people out of here." I gestured at the prepped patients. Then we can keep looking."

"We'll find him," she said. "Don't worry."

While I was busy almost dying, Gawen had defeated his foe and begun loading up warpers onto stretchers.

"Don't forget to give the warpers their shot," Jules called.

Gawen looked up but shook his head. "What?" He blared. "I can't hear you!" He pointed at his ears. The flash bomb had taken his hearing, but he seemed to be able to see just fine. I took out the tranquilizer device the medic had shown us and gave Cougan a dose. Gawen gave me a thumbs up. "Got it!"

Quickly, we got everyone onto their stretchers. Gawen was able to load them on his own, but Jules and I had to work together. Still, it didn't take long. When everyone was loaded Gawen ran to prop open the outer door, while I held the surgical entrance open and Jules dashed around the room, pressing green buttons one-by-one, sending the stretchers back to medics.

As the last made their way towards him, Gawen yelled back to me and Jules. "I'm going with them. I need to make sure they get there okay. Plus, that last guy, he got me pretty good!"

"What happened?" Jules yelled, just I shouted, "You're hurt?!"

Gawen pointed to his ears again, letting us know he still couldn't hear, but I didn't need an answer. I could see the blood dripping down his arm, white bone gleaming inside where the warper had sliced open his shoulder. The cut was deep but Gawen looked exhilarated.

I stepped forward, ready to heal him myself, but the door was already shutting, Gawen's form sprinting into the sunlight.

"Dammit. I could have healed him," I swore.

"It's better this way. He couldn't hear anything, anyway. Maybe I shouldn't have used that flash bomb. You're okay though, right?"

"Yeah, I'm fine. Don't apologize, you saved my life back there."

The building shook, a loud boom I didn't need ears to hear. It was the kind of sound you felt deep in your bones, all through your body.

"What the heck was that?" Jules exclaimed.

"I don't know. You should go with Gawen. It's not safe here."

"And you think I'm going to just leave you? Forget it. Come on, let's go find Khai."

We raced back through the surgical prep room without pausing. In the short amount of time that I'd been standing outside in the hall, I'd felt my powers returning. I wasn't about to stop and let them get drained again. I slammed a shoulder into the double doors on the other side of the room where Cougan and his friend had come in through, pushing them open as I ran.

Emerging into pure mayhem.

Fae fighting against warpers. Patients, some cowering, some fighting, too. I could see my mother trying to calm someone in a hospital gown, the gowned woman beating her arms against my mother's chest. I didn't understand.

"Why are they fighting?" I murmured to Jules. "Doesn't she want to be rescued?"

David's words came back to me. *They're building an army. Capturing and mind-warping more innocents every day.*

"Odin's eye!" I spat. "They've already mind-warped them. These fae, starseeds, whoever they are. They aren't old and weak like Reenah's parents. They're being groomed to fight for the warpers!"

My mom spotted Jules and me. "Girls! What are you doing here? I told you to stay with the medics!"

Each word was punctuated with effort, her breath heavy as she tried to contain the woman pushing against her. I decided to answer her question with one of my own.

"Where's Khai?" I asked as I ran towards the mind-warped woman, sliding and swiping out her legs from under her, cuffing her in two quick moves. "Have you seen him?"

Mom rubbed her chest, trying to catch her breath. "Not yet." I took her hand, channeling healing energy towards her torso as she spoke. "He may not even be here."

"He has to be. What was that loud boom we heard? Maybe it was Khai."

"Hollis," she corrected me, pointing to the far end of the hall where several guards lay under a pile of rubble next to a small crater in the floor. My father was fighting two women, keeping them away from Hollis as my brother straddled a man, cuffing his arms behind him.

"Ah." I released her hand. There was no time to talk. Even as we spoke, more warpers were running through the doors. Grabbing one of my last stretchers, I rolled the small female patient aboard, en-gelled her and pressed the green button. Immediately, the gurney lifted and set off down the hall, bumping against the doors several times before they eased open and it disappeared from sight.

The new influx of warpers seethed with anger, overloading my senses. The hate poured off of them so strongly it almost knocked me over. Thank the gods, Gawen wasn't here. I wasn't sure he'd have been able to fight through it, given how much stronger his empathic abilities sometimes seemed than mine.

"Go help Hollis," she said. "We need to get people out of here before this turns ugly."

"On it." I turned to face the new wave of warpers, ready to throw up a shield wall of counter-emotions but froze when I saw Khai running towards me. My heart leapt, making it hard to speak. Then, I realized that he wasn't smiling.

He wasn't happy to see me. To see any of us.

The auric cloud around him was as dark and forbidding as the warpers and suddenly I wondered what he was doing here. Why the warpers had brought him right to us, why now? A more thorough scan revealed that the newest group of antagonists weren't warpers at all. They were fae, just like us. Except not like us. Not at all. The light fields around them had gone dark, infected with crackling disturbances, flares of hate and jealousy. I'd never seen a person suffering from Ebola, but I had a feeling that if emotions could look like diseases, then these people had contracted the most horrific, endemic death of all good feeling. Whatever the warpers had done to them, the fae here didn't look on us as rescuers.

We'd become the enemy.

Chapter 17

As he ran towards me, Khai's fists began to glow, sparks flying off them.

I should have knocked him out. Raised a shield wall. Something.

But I couldn't. All I could do was just stand there. He raised one hand launching a shard of electricity towards me, and still, I couldn't move. I watched the blue light coming towards me, stunned into inaction. At the last possible moment, something impacted my side and I was thrown out of the way. Behind me, the wall exploded in a cloud of sulfur and dust.

"Dammit, Ana, what the hell are you doing?" Jules yelled in my face.

"He tried to kill me," I said.

"Yeah, I noticed." Like a claymation movie, the dust rose and cemented itself back together, forming a wall between us and the warpers. "Get yourself together. You can do this." Another blast sounded, and Jules swore. "I gotta help Hollis. Be careful."

And then she was gone. She was gone, and my mind was returning. Realizing what had just happened. "He tried to kill me," I repeated. This time, anger tinged my voice.

I crawled to the edge of the small shield wall Jules had made for us and glanced out. Khai was fighting two fae at once. Both air fae, they seemed to be wasting most of their energy on confusing, rather than hurting, Khai. But that would never work. Not with the Khai I knew. A typical fire fae, he almost never got run down, never gave up, never ran out of energy. If anything, they were adding fuel to his fire, their air defenses riling him up, making his attacks more virulent. Soon, he might really hurt someone. And when he did, if he ever came back from this, I knew he'd never forgive himself.

He had to be stopped.

"Khai!" I shouted, rising. "Stand down."

He looked at me and the two air fae paused, backing away. For a moment, I thought maybe he did recognize me, after all. But then he shook his head.

"Nobody calls me that. My name is Kyle. And you people don't belong here."

"You're wrong," I yelled over the noise, coming out from behind the wall. "You're name is Khai. We're here to save you. To save all the fae." I took a step forward.

"Fae? I'm no fae." He sneered.

That threw me. He wasn't just mind-warped into believing he was on their side – they'd made him believe he was one of them? Gods help me. Now what?

"You are. Just like me, like all of us. Your parents, they're waiting for you-"

"My parents are dead. They died at the hands of your people, the so-called Light," he denied.

"No, they didn't. I can prove it to you. Just come with us, and you'll see. I can show you pictures, letters, so much Khai. I've known you since I was born. We took our first steps together. Hell, we used to bathe together."

"Lies." Fire flashed behind his blue eyes and I knew I was running out of time.

"Look, I know Cougan's been messing with you, but I swear-"

"Cougan? What have you done to him?" Balls of blue flame ignited in both his palms.

"Everybody out!" my father yelled.

Time was up. But I wasn't going anywhere. Not without Khai.

I breathed deeply, calling up my own auric shield, locking it in place. He hurled one ball at me, but I'd seen it coming and launched into a lasair spin, just barely dodging the fire. Instead, it splashed onto the floor, melting the wall behind me. I don't know what temperature Khai's flames were burning at, but I knew I didn't want to be anywhere on the receiving end of one.

"Can't we talk this out?" I asked reasonably, though I was quaking inside as I edged towards the doors he'd come in through. Over his shoulder I could see loaded stretchers floating away, returning to the medics. Our people were leaving, just as they'd been ordered, limping after the stretchers. Soon, only Hollis, Jules and my parents were left. My mom was holding her side, her other arm hanging at an odd angle by her waist. Broken, I thought, not needing to read her energy to see what was in front of my own eyes. Some ribs, too, probably. My father carried a man draped over one shoulder. One of our own, judging by his gear and lack of restraints.

"It's okay," I said, nodding at my Dad. "Go. I'll catch up."

He shook his head, starting to drop the soldier to the floor. Khai's eyes widened, realizing there were more fae to fight, and he whirled, throwing another ball of flame at my parents. My mom pushed my father out of the way, screaming in pain as her bad arm took most of the impact. The unmistakably unpleasant smell of burnt hair filled the room as the ball just missed hitting her head-on, singing the ends of one braid instead.

"Hey, Khai! Eyes on the prize, okay? Look at me." He turned back, eyes wild and unfocused. Hollis and Jules crept forward, possibly thinking they could take him from behind. I could see my mother and father arguing. My father, pointing at me; Mom, clearly insisting he take the unconscious fae to safety. My father, shaking his head and poking her in the ribs, making her flinch. She stood her ground, no doubt saying she was fine. I knew, because its what I would have done.

Khai threw sparks of lightning all around me and, frantic, I pushed out with my aura, trying to knock him off his feet. He stumbled, ever so slightly, and laughed.

He laughed.

Memories of Khai laughing as we sparred flooded my brain, and I knew, just knew that he was still in there somewhere. I just had to find him.

I looked back at my mom, saw her sway. My father, grim-faced, supporting her with one arm. Looking at me. Shouting something to Hollis about containing Khai. And then they left, my father somehow managing to carry the weight of all his burdens.

He'd finally done it. Finally trusted me to take care of myself. Well, Hollis, too, but still. Was it wrong of me to wish he hadn't left, that he'd stayed and saved the day? Because part of me really, really wished he had. I wasn't so sure anymore that I could actually do this.

I didn't have time to wallow in wishes, however. Khai had turned, hearing my father's shouts, and watched the doors swing shut behind my parents. Now, he was refocused on Jules and Hollis. Hollis, who was yelling his name, drawing his ire.

"Khai! What the hell are you doing? You don't want to hurt Ana. I know you, man. Whatever they did to you, you're stronger than this. Fight it!"

Khai howled in rage, his skin gleaming in the firelight that danced above his palms. "You don't know me! But you're right about one thing. I am strong. You want a fight? You've got one!" He growled, hurling flames towards my brother and Jules. Relentless, he didn't stop with just one or two balls of fire, but continued on, the blue and white flames coalescing into something huge, horrifying. Spreading across the floor like a hungry centipede, racing towards my brother. Jules screamed and threw out her hands, rearranging the walls on either side of her, drawing them in to form a thick barrier between them and the flames.

Between them and us.

"Ana!" Hollis yelled. Beyond the huge wall Jules had created, above the roar of the fire, I could barely hear him. But I could feel his anguish and fear.

"Nice to know you really care, bro," I whispered. Watching the fire leap and grow, I knew there was no way they were going to make it back through. The hallway clouded with smoke, making me cough. This place was turning into a death trap.

Khai turned to face me.

"Looks like it's just you and me now," he said, grinning demonically.

Chapter 18

"I don't know, I think you might be a little too hot for me," I said coyly, shrugging one shoulder as I took a step back.

I thought about the exit behind me, fresh air so close on the other side of the doors. But I wouldn't, couldn't, leave Khai.

"Am I really worth all this?" I asked. "Are you actually willing to burn, just to kill me?"

"Die killing a fae? Absolutely. You people ruined my life. I could have had parents, lived a nice normal childhood. Instead, you had to take everything away from me."

"So what? Now you're going to just kill me, burn for them? For people you never knew?" I coughed, shaking my head. "You'd be dying for nothing. Your parents are alive, Khai. The only people who have tried to hurt you are the warpers – people like Cougan. Not me. And I can prove it."

Closing my eyes, I allowed my senses to snake out, dowsing for water. You'd have thought there would be a sprinkler system in the building, but no. The Warpers didn't care if their patients died in a fire. But they did care about cleanliness. And the inlet pipe for the bathroom at the end of the hall just happened to run through the walls of the hall.

Eyes flying open, my lips twitching to one side in a self-satisfied smirk, I summoned all the water in the building. Calling it to me, bending it to my will. The water main groaned, and then it exploded, bursting through the wall and spraying everything. Flames were doused, smoke settled, only to be replaced by a fog of skin-searing steam. Still, the water continued to rain down over us. At least the alarm had finally been silenced, probably shorted out by the water.

Growling, Khai ran at me, fighting me like the fae he was. He might have believed he was a starseed warper, but his body knew differently. He'd been training to be a Light Guard for months, learned martial arts growing up right alongside Hollis and me, and his moves betrayed him.

"Do you know what that is, what you're doing?" I asked, ducking to avoid his legs as they vaulted over me, narrowly missing my head.

He didn't answer.

"Lasair, Khai. It's a fae fighting style. How do you think you learned it?"

My question distracted him for a moment, just long enough for me to deliver an open-palmed punch to his solar plexus. He stumbled back and I grinned, moving in, spinning at the last moment to jab my elbow into his side and dance behind him.

"Cougan trained me in Capoeira," Khai snarled, whirling to face me.

"He did not," I said, exasperated. Khai punched out at my face, lightning fast. It was all I could do to avoid his fists from connecting. He was so much bigger than me, I needed to knock him out. I couldn't last much longer. But when I reached for my power, it wasn't there. I'd done too much, drained my resources. Calling up the water had used up everything I had. One of his punches got past my own, clipping my left ear. Dazed, I shook my head, trying to clear my vision.

At least I wouldn't burn to death. Maybe it wouldn't be so bad, letting Khai capture me, turn me into one of them. At least I'd be with him.

Okay, where had that thought come from? Now I knew I was getting into dangerous territory. Let myself get captured? It'd never happen. I needed to do something. How did the starseeds deprogram their people when they got them back? Did Callie have some sort of secret weapon, or what?

Thinking of Callie, I suddenly remembered the crystal shard she'd given me. Could it help?

I dropped to the floor and rolled between Khai's legs, kicking up into his crotch as I went. My foot made contact with the hard inner muscle of his thigh, going wide of soft central target I'd been aiming for, but I decided to consider it a win.

Doubling over in pain from what had to be a really nasty charley horse, Khai's attention was off me for a moment. I scrambled to my feet, digging in my pockets for the small starlit shard Callie had given me. Had I lost it? Finally, my hand closed around a thin, warm object. The stone. Triumphant, I pulled it from my pants and pointed it at Khai, willing something, anything to happen.

Nothing.

"Come on, damn you!" I shook the crystal in my hand, trying to wake it up. How did this thing work, anyway? Callie hadn't been able to do anything with it – why did I think it would do something for me?

I screamed, frustrated, clenching the stone in one hand and just wishing, praying, it would do something.

It didn't.

By this point, Khai had straightened. Static electricity flickered weakly around him, just enough to let me know he was trying to call up his powers, too, and failing. Still, he smiled like he'd won.

Gods, how I wanted to smack that look off his face.

"Dammit, Khai!" I yelled. "Stop being such an ass! Don't you get it? We came here for you, and we're not leaving without you. We love you, okay? I love you!" I started to cry, tears coursing down my cheeks. "You don't know how worried I've been..."

Heat seared my palm, and I gasped, dropping the crystal. On the floor, it glimmered and shone, so bright I started to wonder if it was going to melt through the floor like one of Khai's fireballs.

"Love is the key that unlocks all doors, transcends time and space. It is the wave of light on which we ride, the tenor of the voice of creation." A deep chorus of voices rang echoed through the hallway. The lights above us sparked and flickered, keeping time with the choral tones.

"Ana? Who is that? What's going on?" Hollis yelled. Distantly, I heard him ordering Jules around. "Help me, put your hands here. On three!"

There was a countdown, barely audible above the din of otherworldly voices.

"One."

"We are the Nommo. We ride forth on love-"

"Two."

"-and light. Your light calls to us, and your love. Soon we will be there. But for now, let your pain be no more. Be one with the light-"

"Three!" Jules and Hollis shouted together, and the wall Jules had created split apart, turning to dust as if it had never stood in the first place. Eyes wide, I looked at them, watched Hollis search the area for the source of the voice. Wordlessly, I pointed at the crystal.

"*-and allow your love to rise.*"

"Screw love," Khai muttered, "and screw your fae party tricks. The Nommo are dead."

He squatted down to pick up the crystal. The moment he touched it, light flooded the hallway. The crystal glowed in his hand like a thousand high-beams. He had a moment of pure, priceless confusion etched across his face, and then a ring of light blasted through us all, with Khai at its epicenter. Landing on his butt with his legs straight out, it was almost comical the way he flew backward towards the wall. At least, it was until I heard the dull thud of his head hitting the concrete, and watched his eyes flutter shut.

The crystal fell from his limp hand, lifeless now, dark and still on the floor. Just like Khai.

"Khai!" Even though I was closest, Jules and Hollis arrived at Khai's body the same moment I did, their long legs reaching further, faster.

"He can't be dead," Hollis whispered, looking stricken.

I cupped Khai's cheek, then ran my hand down his neck, searching for life.

"His pulse is weak, but he's still here." *Barely*, I thought, but did not voice the word aloud.

I picked up the stone, shoving it back in my pocket and reached for my power, hoping I could summon even a fraction of my regular healing abilities. Surprised, I felt them flood though me. The Nommo's stone packed a good dose of light, it seemed. Though maybe as a water fae my power wasn't just fueled by light – maybe it had just as much to do with emotion. With love, like the Nommo had said. All it had needed was a little boost, that was all. Closing my eyes and thinking of that beautiful bright crystalline light, I placed my hands on his chest, funneling all of it into him, every last drop.

"Ana, you're glowing," Jules said in awe.

I opened my eyes, prepared to protest, but she was right. Pure cobalt light was radiating from beneath my hands, casting an eerie glow around us. I wasn't sure what was happening, but I wasn't going to stop now. Not until I had brought Khai back.

Frowning in concentration, I sent every drop of love I had into that light. Every moment I'd missed him, every bit of guilt and worry I'd felt after I'd escaped Aeden.

Still, his eyes remained shut.

I closed my eyes again and reached deeper. Remembered the moments we'd spent teasing each other on the Long Trail. The first time he'd bested Hollis in a fight, tasing him as they rolled down my back porch stairs in a tangle amid thunder and rain. How he'd looked as he'd bounced to his feet, triumphant. Glowing. Khai in perfect health and joy. The look on his face the next night, when he'd pulled Slice off of me mid-kiss: expression stormy, his normally blue eyes literally popping with flashes of silver light. He'd been furious with me, forced me into the car, brought me home. He'd insulted my party clothes, tried to make me feel bad about getting drunk on 'shine, but I'd gotten the drop on him.

"Knocked me right off my feet," a deep voice murmured.

My eyes flew open. Khai's eyes weren't just blue anymore, they were pure cobalt orbs, like my hands. Except... My hands weren't glowing anymore. The power had shut off, like an automatic faucet. He was full, and the light show had ended. Except-

"Your eyes," I whispered. Khai reached up and put a hand over mine.

"I remember how mad you were that night. You thought I was making fun of you. That I didn't approve of how you looked, how you'd dressed up for Suki's party. But that wasn't it at all. I was scared."

"Scared?" His words didn't make any sense. I could barely wrap my head around the fact that Khai, our Khai, was really back. It hit me that somehow he had seen the memory I'd been tapping into. Maybe all the memories. How?

He nodded and then winced a little, like moving made his head hurt. The light in his eyes was starting to fade, but his gaze remained laser-focused.

"Scared." He struggled, pushing himself up to sit straighter. "When I saw Tim bringing you drinks, and then Slice with his hands all over you... I didn't want anyone to see you the way I'd always seen you."

"What, like your best friend's clumsy sister?" I joked.

"No, Ana," he brushed the pad of his thumb over my lips and I froze, shocked. "Like my hot best friend. The girl I've always been too scared of losing to hit on. The only person I know who can kick not just my ass, but my heart."

Jules whistled, and I was dimly aware of her tugging on Hollis, pulling him away from us.

"Me?"

"You," he confirmed.

I couldn't believe it. How could I not have known? And then, I felt something inside me start to crumble and fall apart, like Jules' wall of dust. A part of me, maybe the same part that had kept my water abilities hidden below the surface for, had also been shielding me from my own feelings so effectively that I hadn't even realized. Little Ana. Awkward Ana. I'd shoved down every feeling of being good enough for such a long time, I'd closed off part of myself. I'd never expected to measure up to the rest of my family, not really. So I'd boxed myself in. Now, with a flood, the dam inside me burst, and in its place the surge rushed in. Suddenly, I could feel everything that Khai was saying and more – all his emotions, all his love.

I gasped for air, my eyes searching his, and then I was in his arms, somehow having found my way onto his lap, and every self-deprecating thought I'd ever had about being too small was banished forever because here I fit just perfectly. Here, everything was right. And I could tell that Khai thought so too, because his lips were crashing into mine and his emotions rocked through me like waves and then I wasn't just feeling, but seeing, actually seeing. Suddenly, I wasn't just kissing him here, in the hallway of a renovated pig shed. We were in my parents' basement, surrounded by older boys and girls, kissing for the first time. He was nervous, so nervous. So scared to do it wrong, so afraid that I would laugh at him. Even then, he'd loved me with a depth that made it hard for him to breathe.

How had I never known?

I'd looked up at him, so young and trusting, hands on my hips with a glare in my eye. Seeing myself through his memories, I realized I looked small, but fierce. So he'd kissed me, not because I'd threatened to tell Mom and Dad if the boys didn't let me play spin the bottle, but because he'd never wanted anything so much.

Until now. Because now the surge was flooding through both of us, coming in waves. I moaned, and he trembled in answer. I ran my hands down his muscled arms, then moved on to the hem of his shirt, ready to pull it over his head.

Someone coughed. I ignored them, intent only on getting closer to Khai. A hand grasped me under my armpits, hauled me off of Khai. I readied myself to fight, came up with arms swinging. I had to defend Khai. And Hollis, and Jules. Were they okay? Slowly I came back to myself, back to my surroundings.

Realized it was my Dad and Hollis, both holding me at arms' length now. I flushed. They'd seen all that?

"Wish I hadn't" Dad muttered.

Crap. Had I said that out loud? I blushed more fiercely. Khai rushed to his feet, stammering.

"Alec! I mean, sir," he trailed off as my father glared at him. "Sorry, sir," he said sheepishly. My father stared at him a little harder, then relented. "Come here, son. I'm glad you're back with us. Had me worried there for a minute." My dad pulled him into a hug, patting him on the back.

If he was patting him a little harder than he should of, hugging him a little too tightly, well, who could blame him? We'd all been worried about Khai. Now, he was back, healthy and hale, and it seemed my father had something new to worry about.

Chapter 19

Unable to stop smiling, I helped Jules finish loading up two more warpers onto the stretchers, sending them outside. Despite his protests, my dad had strapped Khai on one, saying Claire would kill him if he didn't see him properly taken care of. I knew Khai was in perfect health, better than, actually, but I also knew better than to argue with my dad. I was pretty sure he just wanted to get Khai as far away from me as possible. If it made him feel better, I was okay with letting my dad have his way. For now.

Looking around the empty hall, I grinned at Jules.

"We did it. We really did it."

"Looks like it," she said. "So, when were you planning on telling me you had a thing for Khai?" She slapped a hand on my back, reeling me towards her as we walked out into the late afternoon sun.

"There was nothing to tell." She looked at me, skeptical. "No! I swear, I had no idea." I laughed, surprising myself with the clear joy of the sound, because really, I hadn't known. And how ridiculous was that? "I think the better question is, how could you not have told me? There must have been signs."

"Sometimes... I thought maybe. But then you'd go back to being you, so involved with your books and everything. I figured I was just imagining things. And I never had a clue he liked you. I should have noticed something was up when you guys started fighting on the trail. I was just so caught up with my own drama with Hollis." She sighed. What am I going to do with your brother?"

"Whatever you want," I laughed. "He's *all* yours."

Jules chuckled. "Yeah. I think he just might be, after all. It's kind of scary, you know?"

"What?"

"Getting what you've always wanted." She pointed at a nearby sapling and the branches lowered in deference, bowing towards us. "I never imagined I'd really get to have powers, like you guys."

"I didn't know you wanted them," I said lamely, feeling like a bad friend.

"Who wouldn't?"

"Well, for what it's worth, I always wanted what you had – long legs, a fast pace. I always felt so slow and awkward next to you."

"Well, aren't we just a pair of idiots?" she laughed. "And now we both have what we wanted."

"Minus the legs," I allowed. "But you know what? I think I'll take Khai instead." I giggled, still having a hard time believing that this was going to be my new normal.

"So what the hell happened back there, anyway? Where did all that light come from? When you held out your hands towards Khai, I thought you were going to burn a hole through him. I'm still seeing spots. And that voice – sister, you sounded full-on possessed. Seriously, you scared me."

"It wasn't me. It was this." I pulled the dormant starseed shard from my pocket. "The crystal Callie gave me. The Nommo saved him, not me."

"Well, you did something. It wasn't all them. That blue light coming out of your hand, and his eyes. That was amazing. But promise me, if I ever need healing, you're not going to go all romantic on me, too," she teased.

"You wish you could be that lucky." I sighed. "No, I have a feeling the only person I'm going to be kissing from this day forward is Khai."

"The surge?" Jules whispered. "Did you feel it?"

I looked around to make sure no one was nearby. "Hoo boy, did I ever."

Jules threw back her head and laughed. "We can have a double wedding!"

"Oh please, let's not go there just yet. We still have to get through school. Heck, we still have to get out of warper territory." I pointed at the field before us, where medics were overseeing the loading of several ships. "Looks like we needed those extra transports after all. Good thing Callie planned ahead. Do you know if they found that guy, Cliff Collet?"

"I don't know. Let's go ask." There were hundreds of injured warpers and starseeds floating by, filling the four starseed ships. By comparison, we'd obviously had it pretty easy in the fae labs. Looking around, I spotted Joaquin by one of the ships, checking over each patient as they passed.

"Joaquin!"

"Hey girls," he said, looking up with a distracted smile. "Glad to see you made it out alright." Then, his brow furrowed. "You shouldn't have run off like that, you know. Mrs. Alvarsson's already chewed me out for not keeping a better eye on you."

All too late, I realized what his assignment had really been: babysitter.

"Sorry," I said, trying to look it. "Hope you're not in trouble."

"Nah. Callie warned me what might happen. She said not to get in your way."

"She did?" I asked, surprised.

"Yeah. She's awesome, isn't she?" I detected some pretty rampant hero worship in his tone, and wished I knew more about Callie's history. Maybe someday I'd get to hang out with her more.

"The lady's still got it," Jules agreed. "Actually, that's why we came over here. Do you know if they found her friend, Cliff Collet?"

Joaquin scrunched up his face, thinking. "Collet, from the Montreal office? Can't say I've seen him." Seeing our faces fall, he shook his head. "Doesn't mean he wasn't here, though. He could be on one of the other ships. Let me check the med-logs." Quickly, he started tapping away on his med-tab, bringing up the logs. "No, nothing. Oh, wait, here he is! Just got logged on Delta ship. See over there?" He pointed across the field, to the largest transport. "That's his stretcher heading into the ship now."

"Is he okay?" I asked hurriedly. I don't know why, but the idea of him not making it back to his husband wasn't something I was prepared to handle.

"Let's see...looks like he was mind-warped, but that's nothing we can't fix with some TLC. Minor concussion, two fractured ribs, burns to the left arm..." My heart hammered, hearing the injuries, but Joaquin looked up at us and grinned. "He's gonna be fine." Seeing our faces, his own smile faded. "No really, trust me, he's going to be okay."

"You're not just saying that?" Jules asked.

"No, definitely not. I promise!" he reassured us, seeing the skepticism on our faces.

"I'd rather see to him myself," I heard the words leave my lips before I'd even thought them.

"Not happening, sorry. Transport's leaving." Delta's medics were retreating up the gangplank, the doors sliding shut behind them.

I swore under my breath, irritated that I'd missed the opportunity to meet Cliff face to face. Somehow, I felt like I knew him, even though I'd only seen the moments of his capture through a memory left behind, nothing more.

"Don't worry," the medic said. "We have the best docs around. He's gonna be fine."

"Better than a fae healer?" Jules asked tartly.

"Better than-? Oh. I see. Our docs don't work quite the same way, no. But he'll be fine, I promise. Don't worry," Joaquin repeated. "Delta's on its way to Ithaca right now."

"Ithaca?" I asked, scanning the sky. Already the ship was out of sight. Or maybe it had simply re-engaged its cloaking device so as not to upset any local sky-gazers. "I thought it was heading back to Boston."

"Nah. Boston's gonna have its hands full with the warpers we're sending them. Everybody else is headed to our team at Cornell."

"You guys work with Cornell University?" Jules asked, surprised.

"Honey," Joaquin giggled. "We *are* Cornell University." He glanced at his med-tab and sobered up. "You girls better get going. Looks like all transports are getting ready to leave. Local law enforcement are headed here after some noise complaints, and it's better if we're not around when we get here."

"But they'll know something's happened, right? I mean, come on, it's pretty obvious, isn't it?"

Joaquin shook his head, shooing us away. "We've got it all under control. Gregors has been cleaning up the warpers' messes for centuries. Now go!"

He turned and headed up into the ship with the rest of the ground crew. Jules and I took off, running for our ship. Joaquin was right. The steady stream of stretchers and teams had all boarded, we were the last ones in the field. Mom was standing at the foot of our ship, watching us approach.

"I was just about to send your brother after you," she said, head wagging. "Come on, we've gotta jet."

"Sorry," I said, following her up the walkway. "I was trying to see Cliff, Callie's friend."

"I get it, you want to make sure everybody's taken care of. But it's my job to make sure you're taken care of. Okay?"

"Sorry, Mom."

Safely inside, she punched the button to seal the landing and pulled me close, kissing the top of my head. "I've always said, it's the quiet ones you've got to watch out for." I could hear the repressed laughter in her voice. "But your father insisted Hollis was the one who would give us trouble someday."

"Sorry to disappoint," I mumbled.

"Are you kidding?" My mom pulled back and grasped my chin, peering down into my eyes. "Honey, I am so, so proud of you. You have no idea. You've finally allowed yourself to really be who you are. You've become your own person." Looking satisfied with what she'd seen in my eyes, she released my chin. "You, too, Jules."

"Aw, thanks, Mrs. A." Jules beamed, pleased with the praise.

"I've told you before, call me, Siri. We're all adults here. Speaking frankly, I have just one request of you."

Jules straightened. "Anything."

Mom looked her over, looking serious, and I watched Jules begin to fidget. But I knew my mom. The gleam in her eyes flashed nickel. She'd never been good at acting her age, and the gleam usually preceded a bit of fun.

"Promise me, you'll lead my son on a merry chase."

"Excuse me, ma'am?" Jules said, taken aback.

"Play hard to get. Make him work for you. Everything's always been so easy for him. A little effort will do him some good." She winked at Jules.

Jules bit her lip, trying not to laugh. "Um, okay. I'll do my best, ma'am."

"Siri."

"I'll do my best, Siri."

"Thatta girl." She patted Jules' arm. "Now, if you two will excuse me, I have a husband to kiss."

She strode off, leaving me groaning and pretending puke while Jules sank against the wall laughing.

"I love your parents," Jules said, wiping tears from her eyes. "For real."

"Yeah," I said softly, watching my mother straddle my father's lap and sink into his arms. I shook my head and rolled my eyes. "Me, too."

Chapter 20

"There's Hollis," I said, pointing him out to Jules. His head was bent while he sat at Khai's side. My parents had insisted on keeping him en-gelled him for the voyage, despite both our protests.

"Mmm, you know what? I think I'm going to listen to your mom and give him some space. I'm gonna go check on Gawen. Wanna come?"

I shook my head, unable to tear my eyes from Khai's face, strangely pale and green under the exo-gel.

"He's okay, you know," she said softly. I knew she meant Khai.

"I know."

"Come find us when you're done." Taking my mother's advice to heart, Jules sauntered over to Gawen where he was laughing with a bunch of Light Guards, a big bold smile on her face. Instantly, several of the Guards were offering her their chairs, vying for her attention.

My own gaze wandered back to Hollis. To Khai. I walked over, placing a hand on my brother's shoulder. Was he actually praying? But then he looked up at me, and I saw his cheeks, wet with tears.

I could have teased him. It was within my rights as a sister. I mean, just try to imagine it: Mr. Perfect, the indomitable and unbreakable Hollis Ward, crying. But

Mom was right. We were all adults here. Tears were appropriate, not something to make fun of.

I leaned down and gave him a good, long hug. I didn't have to go far, since sitting actually placed Hollis near my own height.

"Thanks, but you don't need to-"

"Shut up, you idiot." Hollis squirmed uncomfortably, but I didn't let go. I sent a small dose of healing energy through him and felt him relax with a sigh.

"Okay, I guess I needed that," he admitted when I finally released him.

"Doesn't everyone?" I replied lightly, pulling a chair up beside him to stare at Khai while Hollis wiped his face with the back of one hand. Mom had always said that the best way to talk to teenage guys was side by side, while their vision was occupied with something else, like a video game. Khai wasn't nearly as entertaining, but I figured he would do. At least he was visually appealing. "He's going to be okay, you know."

"I know," Hollis said quietly. For a while, we just sat there, saying nothing. When he reached out to hold my hand, I practically jumped out of my seat. Hugs were rare between us – holding hands? I couldn't remember the last time we'd done that, but I was pretty sure it pre-dated his entry to middle school. "I want to apologize."

"What for?"

"Everything. That place back there-" He shook his head, exhaling. "It really opened my eyes. You were right to be mad, at all of us."

"Really?" I mean, I knew it, but I'd never expected him to agree with me.

"Yeah. It was selfish of us to try and protect you. We were so focused on you, we didn't really think about how bad the starseeds had it, how much they needed our help. Of course, they didn't exactly think they needed our help, either," he said wryly. "But they did. What I saw today, that can't be allowed to continue. And you knew that. You wanted to help David, help everybody. You've got a really great heart, Ana. Bigger than mine."

"Well, I could have told you that," I said, laughing. "No but seriously, don't say that. As much as it pains me to admit it, you are a good guy. Mr. Perfect, remember?"

"I'm not so sure anymore. I've been so scared of not being perfect for so long, I've pushed away anything that I thought might make me weaker."

"Like girls you might care about?" I couldn't help asking.

Hollis sucked on his top lip, rocking a bit in agreement. "Gods, Ana, you really don't pull any punches, do you?"

"Not anymore," I said, winking at him. "Speaking of girls, I think I know one that might be good for you."

"Oh yeah," he said, laughing. "Let me guess..."

He looked over at Jules where she was busy being the belle of the ball among Gawen's new buddies and his expression soured.

"Good luck, bro. I think you've got your work cut out for you. But you already knew that, right?"

"Yeah, I kind of did," he admitted. Then his eyes took on a wicked gleam. "What about you? You know this punk has had a thing for you forever, right?"

"You knew?" I gasped, swatting him on the knee.

"Of course, I knew. I see all, know all, remember? You know, he hasn't dated a soul since we've been up at school together. With you guys calling each other practically

166

every day, it didn't take a psych degree to figure out what's what."

"I wish someone would have told me," I grumbled.

"Aw, now how would that have been any fun? Besides, I figured if you didn't want to date Khai, who was I to judge?"

"Point taken." I leaned back and looked at my brother with new eyes. "You know, you're really not that bad."

"Thanks, squirt." He rose and mussed my hair. "I better go stake my claim."

I groaned, trying to straighten my hair. As if it would ever obey my will. "I take it back, you're still a jerk," I called after him.

He laughed, but he only had eyes for Jules as he stalked towards his quarry. Me? I turned back to Khai, silent once more. Warmth spread over me at the thought of Khai dateless in Montreal. I'd been so sure I was the only one with no social life, I hadn't noticed the one guy trying to catch and keep my attention.

I was lost in thought when my chat device lit up, a call coming in. I looked around, surprised. Who could be calling me now? Pretty much everyone I knew was riding here on the same transport. Maybe it was Shania. I hadn't talked to her in weeks, and that had been by mail.

"Hello?" I said, picking up the call.

"Ana?" Callie's face shimmered into view above my chat, her golden eyes shining against the dark backdrop of her skin.

"Callie, hi!" I smiled down at her. Then, I paused — concerned. Why would someone like her be calling me? She had to have her hands full dealing with the incoming warpers and affected starseeds. "What's up?"

"Nothing bad, don't worry," she said, seeing my expression. "I just wanted to call and thank you. I just got off a conference call with my brother, Doug. I can't tell you how thankful we all are for your help bringing Cliff back to us."

"Me? But I-"

"Told us where to find the warpers? Made sure we knew that Cliff was still alive and gave us hope? Yes, you. No use pretending you aren't a hero. Give in with grace. You'd be surprised how much easier everything is when you do."

"Sounds like you're speaking from experience," I mused. She threw her head back, laughing.

"Boy, am I, ever! You have no idea. Or maybe you do. Anyway, I had another reason for wanting to call. My ring – it did something odd earlier and I wanted to check on you. Do you still have the shard I gave you?"

"I do, yes. In fact, it helped me save someone I really care about."

"It did!? How?"

"Khai, he was warped, he didn't remember any of us at all and I thought he was going to kill us but – the stone, I don't know exactly how, but it fixed him."

"Did you hear anything?" Callie asked, breathless. "What did you see?"

So I told her about the light, and the voice, and what the Nommo had said.

"So you mean," she said, "they're still coming back?"

"That's what they said. 'Soon.'"

Callie huffed and shook her head. "Soon. I've heard that before. They said the same thing decades ago. Unfortunately, I have a feeling we have very different concepts of time. I fear I might be dead and gone before they ever get here."

I wasn't sure what to say to that. "Is that why you gave me the shard? In case they come when you're gone?"

"Honestly? No. I didn't really have a good reason for doing that. Just an instinct, you know?" She grinned, and I had a hard time imagining her ever dying. The soul of Calliope Winters was vibrant and feisty. I was pretty sure she'd live a long time yet and told her so.

"I appreciate the sentiment and hope you're right. The Nommo coming back, that's something a girl doesn't want to miss. So, allow your love to rise, huh? That's all they had to say?"

"Pretty much." I shrugged, not about to tell her about what had gone on between me and Khai. Some things were private. Or at least, they should be. "Do you want me to send the stone back with the pilots? After we land, I mean?"

"The shard? No, you keep it. You've more than earned it. Tell your parents they should think about getting it set, though, maybe made into a nice pendant or something. Never know when it might come in handy again."

"I like that idea. Khai's dad is a whiz at metal-work, I bet he could make me something." Already, I was imagining all the possibilities.

Callie smiled indulgently at me. "Good. You have him do that, soon as possible. And Ana? Make sure you keep your guard up. We've won this round, but there are still warpers out there. I swear, sometimes I think the Nommo are already up there, watching us, just waiting for us to clean up our own damned mess before they return. Stay safe, okay?"

"I will if you will," I grinned back at her and she threw her head back again, rich laughter pouring over me like sugar. Behind her, a handsome man with a strong surfer-vibe leaned over her shoulder. "You are a wise young woman, Ana Alvarsson. I like the way you think." He kissed Callie on her cheek. "You hear that, gorgeous? Stay out of trouble, both of you."

And then he was gone and we were both laughing loudly.

"Who was that?" I asked.

"My husband, Ethan," Callie said smiling at someone out of view, I could only assume Ethan. "He's come to drag me down to dinner. I guess I should go." Her face went serious and she pointed at me, stern though her eyes glinted molten gold. "You, young lady, will stay away from warpers, you hear?"

"I will do my best, ma'am," I said, biting the inside of my cheek.

"Good." She winked before she ended the call. "Now get back to school and raise some hell."

Chapter 21

The snow was knee deep. Winter had come early to the Canada wilds, making me glad that the fae patients still slept in their stretchers, cocooned in the warmth of the exo-gel. Airmed herself had come up to oversee the transfer of wounded through the portal. I'd cringed when I'd first seen her, expecting a torrent of rebuke, but she'd barely seemed to notice me. Once I'd realized that she cared more about attending to the incoming fae, I'd breathed a sigh of relief and set about scanning each floating bed as it exited the transport, making notes in the occupant's files for the doctors in Tower Four of Valhalla.

The group by the cave entrance grew steadily as more and more families arrived, looking for their loved ones. One by one, stretchers were hooked up to gravicycles and towed gently below, their patients still en-gelled.

When Khai's stretcher came to me, I hesitated. He didn't need healing. He was perfect, totally restored. I considered what to do, staring down into his peaceful face.

"Ana!" A voice broke out from the cacophony behind me by the tunnels. I turned, catching a glimpse of a waving hand.

Khai's father pushed his way through the crowd, his normally tamed dreads sticking out wildly in every direction.

"Brenin!" I yelled, happy to see him. He held Claire's hand tightly in his as he made his way towards us, grim-faced.

"You found him? You found Khai?"

"I did. He's right here."

Claire gasped, rushing to my side. "Freya's Tears, how bad is it?"

I realized suddenly how it must look: Khai, frozen on the stretcher. Brenin gripped her shoulders, steadying her. Or maybe himself. They must have been assuming the worst. I would have.

"He's okay. Really, he's fine. He was mind-warped but he's completely healed now." Claire stared at me for a moment, processing my words, and then she turned in Brenin's arms, sobbing against his chest. Awkwardly, I rubbed her back, trying to offer comfort.

"Then, why is he being treated like one of the wounded?" Brenin asked, worry creasing his forehead.

"My dad, he thought it safest to make sure Khai was handled with the best care, you know, until you guys could see him." I wasn't about to mention that my dad had probably also wanted to keep Khai's lips off mine while we all shared a ride on the transport.

"Well, we're here now," Brenin said gruffly, his voice thick with emotion. "How do we get him out of this thing?"

"Oh! Um, sure, I can do that, I think. Hang on a second." I rushed to the other side of the stretcher and found the button that had triggered the gelling process. "I think if I just... Yep, there we go." I'd pressed the button, and now the stretcher was humming, the gel evaporating quickly into a fine mist. I undid the harness holding Khai abed and watched him start to wake up. It was a process I'd seen so many times, but never really appreciated. First, his breathing deepened, and then he licked his gorgeously pink lips. Claire had turned to watch, and now she stepped forward, cupping his face.

"Khai? Sweetie? Wake up, Khai, it's your mum."

"Mom?" His eyes fluttered open, clear and blue, his thick dark lashes sweeping the air. "Dad?"

"Yes, son, we're here," his father reassured him. I took a step back, not wanting to intrude on the reunion. "Think you can sit up?"

"Yeah, sure." Khai propped himself up, swinging his legs over the side of the stretcher.

"Don't move too quickly," Claire clucked.

"He's fine, really," I said, unable to help myself. Khai's head whipped around, and his lips parted into a wide smile.

"Ana." Just one word, but it said so much. I saw his aura burst into fire, and I wondered if it was something just I could see. Khai's eyes burned into mine, and then he looked back at his parents. He laughed, the rich sound filling my heart to burst, and I watched him rise. "I'm great, see?"

He leaned down and kissed his mom on the cheek. Claire threw her arms around him, burying her head in his chest as she had into Brenin's just a few moments ago, and then Brenin enveloped them both in his arms, and they were all hugging and laughing.

I watched, unable to tear my eyes away from Khai's.

"Come on, Ana, you get in here, too," his dad called happily. Khai grinned at me, and then I was hugging them all and I knew for sure that everything truly was going to be okay. They were a family again. We all were.

When we came out of the hug, I saw Airmed standing nearby, a small smile playing over her lips.

"Airmed, hello," Claire said, rushing to greet the Ancient. "It's been too long." They kissed each other's cheeks.

"Yes, it has," Airmed said warmly. "I see your son has made it through the gauntlet unscathed?"

"Yes. Isn't it wonderful?"

"Indeed. And Ana, how nice to see you again. I hear you have been practicing your healing work?" Her voice was dry, but her eyes held amusement.

"Yes, she brought me back, in more ways than one," Khai said proudly, slinging an arm around my shoulders, pulling me towards him. Before, I might have bristled at what could have been construed as a protective gesture. But now, I knew it for what it was. Care and support given without a thought. I melted into him, feeling more relaxed than I could ever remember feeling. Comfortable, at last, in my own skin.

"Interesting. And here I thought it was you who was supposed to be bringing Ana back. But I can see that you have both finally learned the lessons I sought to teach. I suppose you will be going back to school now, to begin your studies?" She sniffed as if she thought literary learning was beneath me.

I shook my head. "School can wait."

Airmed's entire face lit up. "So you will return with me to study? There is still so much I would like to go over."

"Actually," I said, looking up at Khai through my eyelashes. "I was thinking I'd join the Light Guard."

Airmed gasped, while Khai let out a loud laugh.

"Your father really is going to kill me now," he said.

174

"Now? Why now?" Brenin asked, looking around for my father. "Khai, what have you done?"

But Khai didn't answer. He was too busy swinging me up into his arms, spinning me around.

"You're crazy, you know that?" he crooned, touching his forehead to mine. "You really want to be a Guard? Because I can lea-"

I silenced him with a hard kiss on the mouth. A solid plant of the lips that turned soft and reassuring. I could hear the sudden stillness around us, and I didn't care. Didn't care about anything except kissing Khai, and letting him know my mind. First, I let the surge carry my thoughts forward on a wave of telempathy. Then, I eased my lips from his.

"I want this. All of it. I want to help the starseeds heal this rift they have with the warpers, for good. And I want to fight at your side, always."

"Odin's Eye. Alec really is going to kill him," Brenin muttered. "First him, and then me." Claire giggled. "Think it's funny, do you? He'll come for you, next. Just you wait and see."

"Hush, you," Claire said. "Let's give the younglings some space." Claire dragged Brenin away, but Airmed stood her ground.

"You must still come and study with me, three times a week," Airmed demanded. By the mouth of the tunnels, Jules waved at me, trying to get my attention, pointing to where Gawen and Reenah were mounting a gravicycle. Together. The sight warmed me to my toes, snow notwithstanding. I gave Jules the thumbs up, urging her towards the tunnels with a wave of my hand, and turned back to Airmed. Out of the corner of my eye I saw Jules climb aboard her own gravicycle, disappearing into the dark behind Reenah and Gawen.

"I would love that," I answered my former teacher, feeling buoyant. She could glare at me all she wanted. I knew she loved me. She'd never have another student like me.

"Then I will arrange for your admission to the Guard. Don't gape at me like that. I can see when a person has answered their calling. I won't be standing in the way of a heart's wantings. Now, I see your father is on his way over here. Khai? Why don't you take Ana to find a gravicycle before Alec encases you in an earthen tomb."

"Yeah, or poison ivy," I giggled. Turning ashen, Khai nodded.

"Good, I will see you both in two hours for dinner." We started heading towards the tunnels but turned back at Airmed's voice. "Oh, and Ana?"

"Yes, ma'am?"

"I'm very proud of you. Both of you." Airmed inclined her head and walked away, stopping my father before he could reach us.

"By the Gods, did we just receive the blessing of an Ancient?" Khai whispered.

I squeezed his hand, felt the surge flow between us, a rising tide of love and home. "Honestly? I don't think I could feel more blessed than I do right now. Come on, let's go home."

"But, I thought we were going to Airmed's," Khai protested as he seated himself at the helm of a gleaming golden gravicycle.

"We are." I climbed onto the cycle behind him, wrapping my arms around his waist, rubbing my cheek against the soft cotton of his tee shirt. If I could have burrowed into him, I would have. I didn't feel like I would ever be able to get close enough to him, get enough of him. It had taken hundreds of miles of hiking, of fighting, of chasing for me to figure it out, but the truth had finally been burned into my heart. "I'm with you. That's home. It's always been home."

Characters & Terms
A Fae & Starseed Compendium

Aeden – The land of the fae within the earth, the origin of all Eden myths and Hollow Earth theories. The word means gifts of fire.

Aho-em – The fae version of "amen."

Airmed – Famous Ancient fae healer, revered as a goddess by some, like so many of the Ancients were. Water fae. Long pale hair, dark eyes.

Alec Ward – Ana's father. Black hair, purple eyes (formerly green and purple, before the Flare). Former Light Guard, now an archeologist hunting Fae Artifacts. Earth Fae, can see in the dark.

Amber Slaight – Former Light Guard, like an aunt to Ana. Eurasian with long dark hair and unique style. Married to Ewan Patterson. Water fae.

Anansanna – The red sun of Aeden at the center of our Earth. Fuels all life on our planet.

Anansanna Alvarsson – AKA Ana. Healer, Water Fae. The second and youngest child of Siri Alvarsson and Alec Ward, both Earth Fae. Female, 19.5 years old. 5'1" with messy chin-length brownish-red hair and green eyes. Named after Anansanna, a fact which she finds embarrassing. Pointy ears. Warm heart, introverted, bumbling and un-coordinated, at least compared to her parents and brother. Hates gym and math, good at writing. Born in late December (Capricorn).

Ancients – Pure-blood fae who lived longer and had stronger powers. Revered as gods by both humans and the newer generations of fae. Few still live today.

Ascensions – Formerly known as Choosings. The ceremony that awakens a faeling's powers on their eighteenth birthday. Before the flare, the ceremony also marked the faeling's alliance with the Light or the Dark.

Aurin – city in Aeden

Ayita – Ana's Fleet.

Bran le Fay – Ana's grandfather, Siri's father. Platinum hair, silver eyes. Earth Fae with special affinity for rocks. Former Commander of the Light Guard. Retired now, enjoying marriage to Frederika Alvarsson.

Brenin Mirro – Well-known artist from Elysielle, married to Claire Brucie, father of Khai Mirro. Long thin dreads, dark black skin, azure blue eyes.

Calliope Winters – AKA Callie. Best-friends with Cliff Collet, foster sister to Doug Rice. Dark, tall and curvy golden amber eyes. Around sixty years old, this former rock star has salt-and-pepper hair streaked with purple and lavender. Starseed speaker, traveler, and reader.

Cala – A blue grass that has an energizing effect when fae come in contact with it. Grown indoor as carpeting in many fae homes, also harvested to use as a rejuvenating juice or milk.

Chat – Flesh colored communications piece designed to rest in your ear, allowing you talk with anyone, anywhere, anytime. Also works holographically for video-communications.

Claire Brucie – Hollis Mirro's mother and Siri's best friend from childhood. Dark curly hair, often sporting colored streaks. Fire Fae. Brucie means forest sprite in French.

Clarise – David Montauk's cousin who went missing hiking the Long Trail. Tall, blonde.

Cliff Collet – Director of the Montreal Gregor offices. Grammer/Glammer.

Dark Fae – AKA Shades, because there is no true dark, only shades of grey. Fae who believed that humans were a lesser race to be used and ruled. Transformed and reformed thanks to Siri Alvarsson in the Inner Origins series.

David Montauk – 29 year old Starseed, searching for his cousin who went missing on the Long Trail. Blonde hair that is long enough to get into eyes, at least in the front. Brown eyes. No siblings. Traveler.

Director Carmichael – Head of the Starseed HQ in Boston.

Dorian Claffsson – Non-nonsense Commander of the Light Guard. Blonde, hazel eyes.

Doug Rice – Calliope Winters foster brother, Cliff Collet's husband. Former Naval JAG officer. Tall, grey-haired, African-American.

Eastie – A high-speed rail system that connects all the major cities along the Eastern States

Elaine Carhartt– Warper Speaker. Curvy build with long silvery hair. Loves to wear white. Dated Marcus

Riley Cougan —One of David's trail mates, a warper and a friend of Tom. Black hair, blue eyes. Dark Irish. Ellen – leader of camp in woods.

Elsa – Colleague of Siri and Alec that finds golden tablets with writing in Capidocchia, translated in Sumerian for Utu.

Elysielle – Artist enclave in Aeden, Shakespeare and Lennon were from there.

Ethan Hale – Starseed, former operative, married to Callie Winters.

Ewan Patterson – Former Light Guard. Tall, lumberjack-looking fae with red hair. Fire Fae. Married to Amber.

Exo-Gel – Medical gel used to keep patients stabilized during transfer, allowing for the monitoring of vitals and supplying oxygen.

Fae – The original creators of planet earth, origins of all fairy myths and legends of the gods.

Farrah Ward – Ana's aunt who was killed as a child during the war with the Dark. Was six, three years younger than Alec, when she died.

Flare – Inner-earth event thirty years earlier when Siri Alvarsson awakened the Tree of Life in Aeden and amped up Anansanna, releasing a flare of light and ions that changed humans and fae forever. Hate fled the world and love rushed in, catalyzing the utopic reality that Ana currently lives in. Wars ended. Technologies shifted. Humans began evolving fae-like qualities.

Fleet – Unicorn-like white horses with horns and manes that fade to black. Built more like ancient horses – heavy bodies, larger heads and huge, prismed, emerald-green eyes. Communicate telepathically with those that can hear them, and will bond with one rider for life.

Flynn Ward – Alec Ward's Dad. Water Fae, Purple Eyes.

Fredrika Alvarsson – Siri's mother, Ana's grandmother. Auburn hair, hazel eyes. Earth fae.

Gawen Black – Water fae, student at McGill, tall, fine and fair with silver eyes. Two years older than Ana, lives on second floor of Jules' apartment building with Reenah. Plays water polo.

Gladiolus essence – Amplifies connection to Anansanna and boosts powers.

Glima –Viking hand to hand style of combat, working much like Krav Maga to get opponent disarmed and on the ground. Used by many fae warriors.

Grammers – AKA Glammers. Starseeds with the ability to glamour appearance and create illusions. Solar.

Gregors – Watcher organization that oversees the training and well-being of starseeds. Run jointly by humans and starseeds.

Gregory Bank – Huge multinational investment bank. Front for the Gregors.

Grey – Warper prisoner. A grizzled, grey-haired man.

Griffin and Mary Black – Gawen Black's grandparents. Water fae, former Light Guard consultants.

GrounSoft – Durable, weather-proof natural synthetic that has the same sort of give to it as a thick bed of moss. Used for range of items, from bus seats to bathroom floors.

Hollis Ward – The oldest child of Siri Alvarsson and Alec Ward. Male. Black hair, silvery grey eyes. 23. Infinitely capable and condescending to his sister. Earth fae. Can talk to animals and gets Visions, hard to surprise. Attends Mcgill University and works in student bookstore. Has silver convertible named Miranda.

Jade Alvarsson – Ana's great-grandmother. "Aunt" Jade. Classy, vivacious, looks fifty, dark hair with one white shock over temple. Lives by Lough Ramor in Ireland, west of Dublin. Earth fae.

Joaquin – Starseed Field Medic.

Jules Harrison – Ana Alvarsson's best friend since grade school, her polar opposite. Tall, skinny, dark as night, and a natural athlete. Great at math. Confident and zany, shy around Hollis who she has a crush on. Birthday in December, just before Ana, making her a Sagittarius. Attending 6-week summer soccer camp at McGill University before the fall.

Kaletka – Siri Alvarsson's Fleet. In Hopi, name means "guardian of the people."

Keith Harrison – Jules' father.

Khai Mirro – Brenin Mirro & Claire Brucie's son, 21.5 years old. Brazilian/latin looking with blue eyes, dark skin. Khai is an Egyptian name, from Claire's time there as a child, meaning "Crowned." Left eyebrow lowers when he doesn't like something.

Lasair – The quick, dance-like martial arts style of the Light Guard. Master this and be a lasrach warrior. Name comes from old Irish word meaning for Flash or Burst of Light

Lifters – Starseeds with the power of telekinesis. Solar.

Light Fae – Light Fae who connect fully with their true nature as fae, the power of Anansanna and the Light. Respectful of nature and all Earth's creatures, including humanity.

Light Council – The ruling body of the Fae, a council of powerful families and elders.

Light Guard – Elite warriors whose original function was to guard the Light Council. Formerly Aeden's first line of defense against the Dark Fae.

Long Trail – Long-distance hiking trail in Vermont, running the 272-miles through state. The oldest long-distance path in the former United States, now connects to Quebec through Canada.

Lochstuppa – A fae herb that promotes inner peace.

Marcus – Montreal Starseed. Dated Elaine.

Mialloch Airron – Member of the Light Council, the governing body of the fae. Grandson of Airmed, a famous Ancient fae healer. Fastidious. Serious. Brown Hair. Brown Eyes. Air Fae. Taller than Alec by a few inches. Godfather to Ana.

Mara – Fae, Reenah Shin's mother, lost at sea and presumed dead along with her husband when Reenah was a child.

Moonshadow – Alec Ward's Fleet.

Niflhelf – Mountain ranges with portal that accesses the forest north of Montreal.

Nommo – Alien race that traveled to earth and bred with humans, creating the star children or starseeds. Their offspring are aligned with the sun or the moon, awakening with abilities after their 28th birthday when exposed to lunar or solar eclipse events.

North American States – A trading nation comprised of every former country from Panama to Canada, plus Greenland

Popigai Crater – Located in Siberia, the carbon-rich site hold diamonds and meteoric remnants scattered over a 62 mile wide site.

Readers – Starseeds with the power of telepathy. Lunar.

Reenah Shin – Air fae, Gawen's roommate, one year younger than Gawen/year older than Ana. Dark hair, charcoal eyes, eyebrow ring. Asian, tall and slim.

Rose David – Druid/Human female. Red hair, funky dresser, avid snowboarder. Close friend to Siri. Married to Maris (same-sex). Works as a country vet and has a knack for herbalism.

Roumkivara – Region famous for their elite horsemen who ride the Fleet.

Ruis – Hollis Ward's Fleet.

Sasha – Montreal Starseed, Elaine's former mentor.

School – Now, all children of earth receive formal schooling for 14 years, from age 5 to 19, and attend free 7-year college programs.

Shania – Ana & Jules friend from high school.

Sharon Schramm – Grey-haired woman. Starseed Doctor.

Sibollae – City in Aeden.

Sienna Cree – Suki Cree's older sister, another girl that likes Hollis.

Siri Alvarsson – Heroine of the Inner Origins series and mother of Ana. Siri means "Marvelous Victory", and Alvarsson means "Elven warrior". Wheaten hair, curly. Tall, thin and fit. Silver eyes. Born in January, Aquarius. Through her Great-grandmother, Morgaine Le Fay, a water fae, she has the ability to heal and to manipulate fate. Through her ancestor Skuld Norna she can see and affect the future, and through the Tyr bloodline, she is honorable and brave, and has the uncanny ability to decide battles. Now an archeologist hunting Fae artifacts with her husband. Earth Fae who can talk to animals.

Speakers – AKA Bards. Starseeds with the power to control minds mind through speech. Solar.

Starseeds – AKA Star Children. Human/alien hybrids with psychic powers.

Suki Cree – Ana & Jules friend from high school, graduation party host.

Tae Shin – Fae, Reenah Shin's father, lost at sea and presumed dead along with his wife when Reenah was a child.

Telempathy – the emotional link between fae who share the surge, channeling their feelings to each other.

Tenzin – Warper prisoner.

Tom – Skinny, Asian. Boyfriend of Clarise. Missing.

Travelers – AKA Walkers or Journeyers. Starseeds with the ability to astral travel and navigate dreams. Lunar.

Tree of Life – Massive ancient tree, almost 1000 feet tall and 144 feet in diameter. The origin of all life on earth, powered by the fusion energy of Anansanna.

Valhalla – the capitol city of Aeden, home of the Tree of Life, the Light Council and the Light Guard.

Warpers – Starseeds who use their abilities negatively for personal gain and/or entertainment, regardless of who it hurts. Unaffected by the Flare.

THANK YOU!

We hope you have enjoyed the Full Disclosure series. Don't forget to leave a quick review somewhere like Goodreads or Amazon – it's the best way to help support your favorite authors.

Want to See How It All Began?

Discover what it was like to be a Starseed before the world changed – start reading **Song Walker**, the first book in the **Starseeds** series.

Or, check out **Shades of Valhalla**, Book One in the **Inner Origins** Series, and meet Siri and Alec before they saved the world.

About the Author

Ellis Logan lives a quiet life in New England, obsessing daily over superheros and the gods of old. She spends her days corralling wild children and communing with fairies. When everyone is settled down and the owls begin to sing, you'll find her typing away and munching on dark chocolate while unseen spirits whisper stories in her ear.

Follow Ellis on Facebook and Twitter at
EllisLoganBooks

Join Ellis's mailing list at EllisLogan.com
to stay tuned for new releases, giveaways
and more!